Voice CATCHER ^{2}

an anthology of
new writing by Portland-area women

Editor: Jennifer Lalime

Second Edition
2007

Voice CATCHER

The VoiceCatcher Editorial Collective

Editor
Jennifer Lalime

Associate Editor
Sara Guest

Assistant Editors
Marti Brooks
Patty Clement
Diane English
Elizabeth Jones
Lilian Sarlos
Jennifer Springsteen
Pearl Waldorf

Contributing Editors
Heidi Greenwald
Emily Trinkaus

Cover Illustration and Book Design
Stephanie Shea, Kismet Creatives, www.kismetcreatives.com
Shannon Bodie, Lightbourne, Inc., www.lightbourne.com
Book interior illustrations, Chuwy, www.istockphoto.com *(altered from artist originals)*

ISBN: 978-1-4303-1018-1

Contents

ONE GODDESS
a once-in-a-lifetime howl

GETTING THERE
imagine how it will go from now on

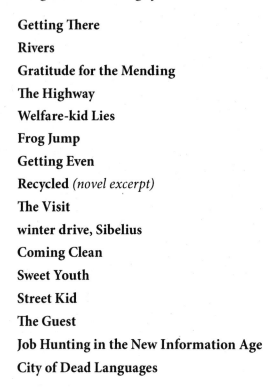

DREAMING YOU
mapping a bare country

ELSEWHERE

the same sky for us all

THE ORIGINS OF

VoiceCatcher

By Diane English

Snatches of voice-catcher (small *v*, little *c*) arrive via a series of nighttime dreams and daytime musings, contained within incomplete scenes, messages and circumstances that reveal themselves over time like pieces of a puzzle doled out one by one. Each time another piece arrives, I try to match it to the previous ones, turning it this way and that, to no avail, until one day, the separate parts coalesce into a whole.

The first of the pieces is a message about spiritual midwifery. I don't have a clue what that means, though my daughter is a Nurse Midwife. She'd once explained to me how midwives view themselves as practitioners who play a supportive, facilitative, nurturing role with women in labor, that they "catch" babies, not "deliver" them. I ponder what that might mean from a spiritual perspective.

Meditating one day to music with a steady drumbeat and the repetitive phrase, *she who hears the cries of the world,* voice-catcher enters my view and refuses to leave. I write a poem about women who hear the cries of the world—the sighs, the stomps and clomps and tromps of feet on our earth—women who catch the joy and pain, the rhythm and music in voices of all kinds. I title it Voicecatcher. The poem eventually feels finished, but the phrase haunts me, appearing over and over again at unexpected moments.

In my weekly writing workshop, I describe how "voicecatcher" won't leave me alone. I refer to its fuzzy connection with spiritual midwifery, and how I have the feeling that I am to do something with it. I surprise myself by suggesting the possibility that I need to be involved somehow in collecting voices of women, perhaps sharing them in print in some way: on flyers in neighborhood newsletters…maybe read aloud in local coffeehouses….

"I'll do the graphics," says one of the women in my writing group. "I'll help distribute the flyers," says another. "We'll help, too!" chime in several multi-talented fellow writers.

I play with possibilities for turning voicecatcher's messages into something tangible. Over a year later, a friend sends me an anthology published by a university press in another state. I am enjoying reading its poems and stories, when what seems like an idle thought enters my mind, "The women in my workshops write every bit as well as these authors."

The thought dances dervishly in my brain and expands, finally demanding to be released to the open air. I meet with Emily Trinkaus, facilitator of the Portland Women Writers' workshops. At the end of most workshops, Emily collects a piece from each participant and prints them into a mini-anthology representing that particular workshop session. I propose to her the possibility of publishing a full-fledged anthology, soliciting submissions from women writers in the broader Portland area. "The time is right," she says, in her understated and deceptively low-key style.

Within thirty minutes of further discussion we've agreed on the general framework for the anthology, and identified five women with whom we'd most like most to work to manifest the vision. All have extraordinary talents and a range of experience ranging from graphic design to technology to editing and marketing. Within a week, we've contacted them. All immediately and eagerly agree to participate. At our first team-planning meeting, the energy and the synergy are palpable. VoiceCatcher is conceived!

VoiceCatcher's first-born edition was published in October 2006 and this second beauty in November of 2007—an offering to the universe from whence came her inception. She was "caught" by a community of readers across Oregon and all over the globe. As with children, it takes a village to raise her, to shape and support her as she grows and develops into full-blown womanhood. Our editors, poets, writers, designers, and readers are her village. In her maturity, she journeys across colorful topography and ever-changing climates, expresses herself in variations of theme and style. Still, VoiceCatcher remains true to her origins—each year showcasing some of Portland's best writing.

Introduction

By Jennifer Lalime

VoiceCatcher exists because a group of women who love to read and write wanted, in the simplest way, to collect the voices of local women and offer them up to the community. The editors of this collection have done very little but read for some months now: cover letters, manuscripts, revisions, and so on. It has been a labor of love.

After sending the last manuscript off to the copy editor, for the first time in many months I opened myself to the world of reading beyond the voices of Portland women. I turned first to a classic I have read many times before and was moved to find such a strong connection between the voices of my contemporaries and George Eliot's words written over a hundred years ago. She speaks in the prelude to her great work *Middlemarch* of the "*meanness of opportunity*" and of the stories of so many women's lives "*which found no sacred poet and sank unwept into oblivion*." I am pleased to tell you that VoiceCatcher has gathered at least a selection of these stories, discovered a number of sacred poets, and presents them on the pages that follow.

We approached this second edition of VoiceCatcher with the same degree of seriousness and excitement as we did the first, but our goal was loftier: create an organization and supporting processes to make VoiceCatcher a sustainable institution. Our vision is nothing short of expecting the women of Portland to line up outside Powell's City of Books each November demanding their copy!

With such stars in our eyes, we planned and we grew. We are a 100 percent volunteer-fueled operation committed to supporting local writers and our mission remains the same: "to offer a publishing opportunity that respects, nurtures and promotes local artists."

On a macro level we began pursuing our 501c3 status to become a non-profit entity, with the long-term goal of being able to pay our authors and editors for their fine work. In the short term, we plan to offer more writing workshops to local women. (The proceeds from our inaugural edition provided scholarships for two participants who had completed Write Around Portland workshops).

On a micro level, we expanded our editorial team, recruited volunteers to support various aspects of our operation, and prepared ourselves to manage double the number of submissions from the previous year. When our deadline fell, our P.O. box burst with over 300 manuscripts. It left us beyond excited and more than a little terrified.

So we come again to the love of reading. It began with the cover letters, introductions to the women whose words our editorial team would get to know over the next several months. Particularly poignant letters were read again or brought to mind throughout this process to remind us of why were ignoring our families, pets, and other duties. One letter from a writer currently serving a prison sentence, stuck with me throughout. She wrote: "*I am aspiring to remain connected to the outside, especially with women of Oregon. As writers, we isolate ourselves, whether it is in a prison cell or on a park bench. If a reader grasps our words we can connect. They hold our anguish and vulnerability in their soul and carry it all over the world.*" We were overwhelmingly lucky to keep so many connections made last year and to forge new ones with writers, editors, bookstores, and readers throughout the city and beyond.

In organizing this year's collection, I looked with confidence, only to the words on the pages before us. Sara and I sat up late one Saturday night with the final selections, the titles of this collection's most unforgettable works on our tongues. Without any hope that this could really be so easy we reviewed each title one by one and watched them fit cleanly into these ideas that became so central to the book you now hold: *One Goddess, Getting There, Dreaming You, Elsewhere.*

To our readers who enjoyed our inaugural edition and for those of you who are finding us for the first time, welcome to our second edition. The stories that fill the pages that follow are now for your soul to carry—around Portland and all over the world.

One Goddess

a once-in-a-lifetime howl

One Goddess

Amanda Sledz

EDDA

Once upon a time Mother leapt fully formed and armor-plated from the forehead of Zeus, sword in hand, a once-in-a-lifetime howl announcing her presence on satellite Earth.

Mother sometimes has the body of a woman and the head of a lion. She crafts her own arrows from found branches and feathers, she smiths her own arrowheads and swords with the fire of Hades and a stolen Thor's hammer. Mother sands the sides of her blades with stone until the striking edge is sharp enough to slice clouds into rain.

One day long ago Mother said to the world that she would be just that: a mother. To preserve her legacy she would only raise warriors.

And so:

Child number one, Dee, ran out of the womb when Mother exhaled.

Her second child (me) procrastinated for two long weeks. I got distracted by the warm rope texture of the umbilical cord, and then I named the afterbirth Charlene and proceeded to tell her everything. Then Mother decided that, dreamer or not, child number two is going to come out. She entered a hospital on her birthday and passed on pain killers to stubbornly embrace bite-a-leather-strap mind-bending agony (minus the whiskey chaser). Mother-masochist forced me into the world completely sober, and with no mind-alteration to make the experience funny, I cried.

Mother said: "You'll be fine. Just fine." So I was.

Three years later Mother and the fates delivered child number three, Rae (she came, she saw, she conquered). Three chasing three created good celestial mojo for another push-and-pop labor. Mother said "go" and Rae stretched and yawned and then walked out laughing and slapping high-fives to the doctors. She already got the joke.

Mother left Dee and me at home with our paternal grandmother when she entered the hospital. When we arrived to get an eyeful of our new sibling

2

and potential competition we were wearing the same clothes Mother left us in. We were dirty and smelly and looked like we hadn't eaten. I don't remember anything of that weekend, and I'm glad.

I do remember seeing Rae for the first time. I had to stand on ballerina-toes to see through the glass. Father pointed to show me which one was three (and I was 3-years-old) and the glass blocked his finger from touching but I tried my best to follow it right to Rae. She was sleeping and sort-of smiling and *poof* I was big sister, so I grew 37 inches to reflect it, though nobody noticed but me.

Mother looked upon her children and thought of all things three, like the three Zorya of Slavic mythology, sitting in the Big Dipper and reining in a giant dog to keep him from eating the world. Their names are Morning, Evening, and Midnight. Mother has all her bases covered.

Mother looked at Dee and me already covering three: dirty, smelly, hungry. She stiffened and knew she must raise warriors. She was there to protect her children; she and no one else.

YEMAYA

The magical age of seven: the number of days in a week, the week it took to complete experiment Earth, the seven layers of heaven observed and recorded by the prophet Muhammad, and there are four seasons and 28 days in each moon-cycle, and seven times four is 28.

I already like numbers.

Every seven days Mother takes us to the library. We can get as many books as we want completely free of charge. When Mother reads she sticks the nail of her first finger in her mouth and props her feet up on the coffee table, and if my legs were a bit longer, I would do this too.

I sit next to Mother, as close as I can without crawling into her lap. I read books my teacher insists are "too hard," but if Dee and Mother read chapter books without pictures, I do too. Compound words are crazy things, two little words hugging each other to try and trick me, but I decipher their riddle. It's the words with punctuation seemingly tossed in at random to create shortened versions of words that were never long in the first place that confuse me.

"Hey mommy, what's this word?" I ask.

"Well," She begins. "What's the first part?"

"Should."

"Okay, well, the next part makes it mean 'not.'"

"It says 'should not'?"

"Close. Shouldn't."

Oh.

I continue reading, sliding even closer to Mother, because I have an idea. If I steal Mother's memories I won't have to ask her so much. I can know every word ever written. Mixed with my own memories I could be wise before Tuesday. I slide close enough to make Mother sweat, and memories pop up along her neck in moisture beads. I gather these drops with my fingertips when she's reading (and not looking), and I place them in my pocket. Later I release the caged memories to crawl up my arm and into my head, and they're so pretty I decide to keep them. I think her memories are just like a slideshow, because no one could appreciate them as much as me. All I want to know is everything.

I sit at Mother's side, stealing, until she sighs and scrapes me off with a spatula.

ATHENA

Mother can sew anything. To make extra money she sews a flower girl dress made of fabric that's not practical and that Mother can't afford, for a girl who lives down the street named Aphrodite. I'm jealous that the puffy-sleeved peach-colored gown isn't mine. Aphrodite knows she looks cute and twirls a circle around my envy.

I want her to bow to Mother and call her the best weaver to ever live before Mother turns her into a spider. She acts like she's a princess and Mother's her peasant, but she'll be sorry when she sees my sisters and me are three and fully capable of fury.

Nine: a magical age of anything goes, three squared, the last of the single digits, the age of the lives of a cat. When you multiply any number by nine the resulting digits add up to nine, as in 9 X 9=81, 8+1=9. Beautiful. There are nine worlds in Nordic mythology, and the Hebrews call nine and her 9-pointed star "the symbol of immutable Truth."

When I am nine Mother shows me how to sew. We select a pattern together after flipping through the bloated design books in the back of the fabric store. She helps me pick out something simple and flattering: a straight skirt with elastic waistband and pockets. The pockets are my idea. I like to hold things: dropped buttons, seeds, receipts, bits of tinfoil, safety pins, memories, tissues for my never-slowing-down nose, and pennies that just might be lucky if given the chance. The verdict comes in at the end of the good or bad day, when I keep the penny or kiss it and return it to the ground in hopes of things turning out better for someone else. The chemistry between each person and each penny is unique.

Sewing the pockets is my favorite part. Merry-go-round and round the pocket turns through the sewing machine, not a straight line but a circle made to exactly fit my hand. I insist on double-stitching the pockets so nothing leaks out. I learn there are lots of things involved with sewing: colored pencils and chalk and measuring tape, patterns and pinking shears and threading of bobbins, loose stitching and tight stitching and hemming and pressing.

We sew a lilac purple skirt (not so princess, but purple is a royal color) with pockets (pockets!) and Mother adjusts the hem to rest just above my knees so I can run and kick like a warrior. I celebrate my skirt by wearing it with everything: button-up shirts with flutter-by necks, T-shirts turned blue from crayon-in-pocket dryer accidents, dressed-up with still-white sweaters Dee used to wear and flat-soled shoes purchased at Payless for under ten dollars.

At school I give a report on how to sew while wearing the purple skirt, complete with visual aids that feature examples of patterns and different types of stitching glued on poster board. I have over 50 notecards and an addiction to feigning expertise. I get an A.

That same day, another child's mother comes in to talk to the teacher about an on-going discipline problem. The somber parent-teacher pow-wow happens during lunch and recess and none of us know what's happening; the accused isn't even invited to his trial. When we get back from lunch mother leads child into the hallway with a "come here" finger gesture women perfect after giving birth. From the hallway comes the sound of smacking and screaming and crying and the whole class falls silent.

The kid comes back into the classroom with his head hanging low, and the mother returns with her face looking sky-falling-gray, and the teacher thanks that mother over and over again: "Thank you so much for coming in, you've really been a tremendous help...." None of us say anything at all.

And we're quiet for the rest of the day, thinking, stunned and humiliated right along with the victim we can't even gossip about, and as we gather our coats to leave the teacher says, "That's much better!" with regards to our behavior that day.

At the age of 9 I know a lot about fury; I know all three of them. I spend the remainder of the school year crushing that teacher's head between my thumb and forefinger every second she isn't looking. I turn her skull to dust while Justice finds her sword, and my sisters and I wipe blood from our eyes and fasten falcon-feather cloaks to our shoulders.

OYA

Mother has many names. Dee and I give her one: Walk-It-Off. We call her this in comic acknowledgement of her motto. To Mother, sickness is annoying, fear is inconvenient, needy is a sibling to burden, and this strange, clingy character should be left alone on an island with a dull knife and a crust of bread for 48 hours to turn sob into howl. I can't go to the bathroom in public for the first 13 years of my life because I'm too nervous. The feeling of father waiting outside and Mother growing foot-tap impatient is enough for me to will my bladder buffalo-sized, until waiting 8 hours is not a problem. Children aren't born with superpowers; they grow them.

Sometime after the hallway incident a counselor arrives at school to analyze and write papers about the big sad eyes of inner city youth. She encourages us in transparent ways to turn in crackhead parents, missing-in-action parents, or nothing-a-good-smack-wouldn't-cure parents. She tells us that every (every!) mother loves her children more than her husband or boyfriend; she has to, because mothers are a child's only defenders. The other kids and I exchange glances.

"Really?" I whisper to one.

"I guess so," he whispers back. I'll have to ask Mother about this.

"Hey mom, who do you love more, us or dad?" I ask while Mother folds laundry and herself to recover from a day of taping gauze over breakdowns as a psychiatric nurse. I'm sort of helping with the laundry, but mostly questioning.

Mother thinks for a second. "I love your father a little bit more," she says.

Oh.

Even gods and goddesses and superheroes have weaknesses, like vanity and envy and kryptonite. Mother has father. I walk it off.

Mother raises warriors. When I or Dee or Rae falls down and scrapes something, we get up. Mother doesn't spray Bactine. She doesn't apply Band-Aids. She doesn't drive to the ER for stitches. Mother says: "Cuts heal if they're allowed to breathe."

CERRIDWEN

Mother plants her children to grow beanstalk big. She waters us with a concoction of Vitamin D milk and aspirin and rose petals and kielbasa, and I grow 300 feet tall. I never have to climb anything; all I have to do is reach. When I stretch the trees turn green with envy. One day I'll ride to school on the back of a bull.

Mother takes me to a library sale, and I don't know how old I am. I know I'm older than seven, because that year we didn't buy anything. Mother cried in the grocery store when other families were buying Thanksgiving turkeys and cranberries that come in a can, because she was taking bread and juice off of her receipt. That day I swallowed her expression and let it leave me full. Her face takes up so much space inside me that while I think about food all the time, when it's in front of me I can never eat it all. Father and Mother call the bits I leave, "bites for the faeries." I think it's a good idea to keep mystical things you only sometimes see happy, and if the faeries eat maybe I will, and Mother won't cry.

This is later than seven, maybe-9, maybe-10, and Mother buys me a book with a worn cloth cover and faded watercolor pictures. The illustrations feature faces drawn with too many angles, experiments of geometry. These characters have two expressions: a closed-mouth smile and an "O!" to signify surprise or anger, depending on the direction of the eyebrows. They hold hands too much and cover their faces when they cry and don't have the good sense to have knees. The book is called, King Arthur and his Knights. I can read on my own, even the words with extra punctuation, but Mother reads it to me because I ask her. I don't pay much attention to the story; my focus is the music box of Mother's voice, the rising of my head as she inhales, the slow drift back to earth as she deflates.

The only character I'm interested in is Morgan Le Fey, because she's got the best name and she's barely mentioned, and so I wonder what her secret is and the best way to ask. All the book says is that she's a witch, which doesn't make her as interesting as what I've already read about witches, like Baba Yaga running around the woods in a house with chicken legs. I wonder about Morgan as my eyes start to close, because I think you need chickens to be a witch. I long for her dark hair and violet eyes (instantly my beauty ideal), and I wonder if I, too, will be omitted from mythologies, as Mother's heart-tempo walks me down to dream.

MOTHER

Father comes home and Mother gets up and my head feels cold and I wish Mother would come back but she doesn't, because like every other day father's mad about something. Mother makes coffee while angry father takes each angry stair one angry step at a time. I think this will give me a few moments before I have to hold my breath again, but he calls me upstairs. He points at a dresser drawer I neglected to close as if it were a bucket of freshly mutilated animals, while screaming something unintelligible. After awhile, all parent-ranting sounds the same; I respond by turning catatonic. My mind drifts to a safe place where swords have names, and lakes have ladies, and I'm only present enough to kneel and close the drawer. Father kicks me in a hard salute; I fall forward to smack knee against cheap, splitting wood. Father storms away to change out of work clothes. I'm bleeding. I'm awake.

"I hate daddy!" I announce to Mother as I head downstairs. It's time for my pocket to open and for the loudest secret hiding there to run.

"Why?" Mother asks. Mother, reach for your armor....

"He kicked me! I left my dresser drawer open, and he kicked me!" Mother, your sword. You mustn't forget your sword.

"Well, why did you leave your drawer open?"

No, this isn't Mother's answer. She's our goddess. I know it. I've seen her face transform from woman to lioness. I have her memories; I gathered them from the back of her neck and placed them in my pocket. Mother, we have the same birthmark. I was born on the same day you leapt from the forehead of Zeus. If you were lost, I'd go all the way to the Parthenon to find you. We have one goddess. Just one. If I know anything, I know this. I know.

Mother?

MORGAN LE FAY

I retreat to the room I share with Rae, pale with defeat. Mother forgot everything when I stole her memories. I must have taken too much. Dee comes in quiet and sits down in front of my dresser. "Look," she says, as she pulls the drawer out all the way. I watch as Dee realigns wood and groove with engineer expertise, and the drawer slides in nice and easy. Dee takes things apart and puts them back together, so nothing stays broken for long. She has super powers, too.

Later father comes upstairs to Band-Aid my knee.

"Do you still hate me?" he asks, after the cut has been covered so it can't breathe and won't heal.

I am nine-years-old, I can go eight hours without peeing, and I am 300 feet tall—yet no one has noticed. Weak and small learn to be clever. Mother hides the face of a lion; I hide dark hair and violet eyes. This self says: Well then. It seems we've found his Kryptonite.

"Do you still hate me?" he asks, after the cut has been covered so it can't breathe and won't heal.

"A little," I respond, giddy at how small father looks from afar. With a mind-altering experience to make the whole thing funny, there isn't any reason to cry.

Reflections on a Quiet Life

Sandra Sakurai

I was not born of slaves, nor did I ride in the back
of the bus. A small town Midwest English teacher's
daughter, I biked home from piano lessons
gathering violets for my mother.

I was not herded into trains, relocated to barracks
in the middle of Idaho after a summer sweltering
in cattle barns in Portland. That summer I played
hide-and-seek, my roller-skated feet riding
waves of a brick sidewalk.

I did not spend my life caring for sick parents
in an old house with shades drawn.
The only child of a deaf mother, I tell
our lip-reading joke about "mince meat" pie,
of being her ears, her voice, sometimes the brunt
of her frustration and anger.

I did not hold three jobs to raise five children
fathered by four men whom I haven't seen since.
I wasn't beaten, abused, didn't run away,
to return, to run again. Though he ran away
from life, off a bridge in Flint, Michigan.
Four years of I do, forty of remembering.

I didn't follow an addiction into chaos
to be thrown, flailed, on the shore
of the rest of life. True to the 50s I cleaned too much,
pleased too many, kept too quiet, asked too little.

I didn't marry and divorce in succession,
abort nor abandon any children. I married a man
of Japanese descent, bore him sons, designed his homes,
his ties, taught him dogs and cream and sugar pie.
I watched depression create another internment.

I could tell of friends and lovers who knew me
how they left me in part or whole.
How I learned to let go, explore new dimensions,
new forms of expression, pushing myself
to my edges, asking others to do the same.

My children do not ask me about my life
or suggest an autobiography. What is there to tell?
Above the Columbia I harvest my life—
gifts of gardens, gathering family, dogs and cats
who romp and run.

Interment

Paulann Petersen

Barrow of rubble. Burial mound
of blown-apart concrete, broken stone
where a bomb struck an hour ago.
In that pile of debris, a mother digs.
With bleeding hands she pulls
at chunks of her family home—
pieces of wall, doorway, roof—
to find the body

this war buried. To pry him
from a makeshift grave.
To wash his limbs with rose water
and wind him in a clean, white cloth.
To keen over the pine coffin
adorned with only that name
she gave him at his birth.
To bury her child
again, in rain-softened earth.

After Finding Out My Sister's Pregnancy is Not

Shanna Germain

For six months, it seems she's swallowed
the moon bit-by-bit, hinge-jawed herself
open in hope of this new growth.

Skin shiny and rivered as washed-up stream stones,
body filling with light-caster, shape-shifter,
weight-bringer—it is hard to remember her shape before.

Grandma handles high weight and declares: girl.
We dig up baby names from memory's moss,
forget that some months the phases repeat.

Last quarter, her belly wanes crescent, empties
to a hollow curve of loss. Even shallow
arcs beneath her eyes hold nothing.

Calendar offers no new illumination.
I turn my face from the blue water pull of
my sister's eyes, hiding the half that knows:

it should have been me. Once, I carried my
regret so low if grandma had seen,
she would have known better than try and name it.

In a dark place who knows what anyone
can see? I thought to be out of reach
of roots, arm buds, everyone else's future.

Greedy, hungry owl, I made a meal
of moon and spit it out, pelleted pile
of half-hearts and bones beneath the family tree.

liberation dress

l. franciszka voeltz

i stitch dresses
of rough fabric
grandma siedlewski wore
in nazi work camps

of summer-thin cotton
from my clothes mom sewed
when i was young

i sew a secret
paper-scrap lining
into hems
containing words from letters
that held me together
postmarked:
minneapolis, spain, chowchilla
san francisco, new orleans, atlanta
letters that carried themselves over continents
letters that passed through bars

each zig-zag stitch
reinforcing the truth
we are so fucking beautiful
we are fierce and strong
we are never alone
threading this message
across landmasses
in infinite languages and dialects
looping
double-knotted
through history

dresses
marked with blood
megaphones
held up against the hush
we've been taught to talk
about our bodies in

we will wear these dresses thin
through daily frictions
of bumping up against

all the times we were
never listened to
or believed
all the times we were told
to shrink back into the
tiny places
we've pushed our way out of
all the times
we wanted to walk and breathe
under the shimmer of stars
alone
but stayed home
"safe"
all the times
we've been labeled incapable
all the times
we've ever been called
pussy
dyke
cunt
whore
slut
bitch

because we said no
because we spoke up
because we kissed each other
because we were just walking past

all the times
we passed on this legacy;
sent it through friend circles
like a secret handshake
set it sailing over bloodlines
like a folded paper boat
cut it into each others' flesh
like an initiation

all the times
we prayed under our breath
for invisibility
and all the times
we seethed unseen

all the times
we've apologized ourselves
back into existence

and all the times
we've ever had to remind you
no matter how high this dress
hikes up my thighs
no matter how low
the neckline lies

this dress
this body
this cunt
are all mine

Frankenstein and Me

Helen Crowley Cheek

E very Sunday morning a flotilla of cyclists in red and black spandex with yellow accents rode past, hunched over their skinny bikes and pedaling in perfect rhythm. I longed to be part of the scene. I was seventy-one years old and owned a beautiful turquoise Browning bike that had been a gift for my thirtieth birthday. With some new tires and a little grease, I, too, could join the world of cyclists. My body was no longer sleek, but I was in pretty good shape and determined not to let the rest of my life go by without adventure.

I entered the Neighborhood Bike Shop timidly. "Just looking," I responded to the nicely muscled young woman who approached me. I checked out the baffling array of clothes and equipment. When I pulled a pair of shorts from the rack I was amazed that they were the exact shape of a bent over body, like the empty shell of a cute butt. To outfit myself with a silky slim shirt and shocking chartreuse or yellow jacket would eat up my clothes budget for a year. I used to ride in just clothes. I didn't need to make a fashion statement. A flyer at the cash register advertised a free class for women beginning cyclists. I thought I knew how to ride a bike, but it had been a long time. I signed up.

The class was held in a grungy upstairs room at the shop. The nicely muscled sales girl, whose name was Patti, took the stage. After a short welcome Patti launched into her spiel. "This is your most important piece of equipment, after your bike of course." She held up an eight-ounce tube of a heavy skin cream called "Butt'r" and proceeded to rub it into the "chamois," a pad that covered the crotch and sits-bones area of a pair of shorts.

"Rub it in good." She squirted more onto her hand and attacked the "chamois" with vigor. "When you get the chamois really soaked then you rub it on yourself."

I crossed my legs self-consciously.

She held up reflective clothes, gloves, brackets for water bottles, mirrors, bells, and lights; white for the front, red for the back. She demonstrated how a helmet should fit and showed us an assortment of emergency tire repair kits.

Riding a bike used to be so simple, I thought.

"Biking shoes are a must." She held up a ninety-dollar pair of stiff shoes with gizmos on the sole that hooked into special pedals. "Toe clips are another option." The information was dizzying. I just wanted to get out and toodle around the neighborhood.

Patti put on a screaming yellow rain slicker and wrap-around sunglasses. "This is Portland," she said. "Be prepared for anything."

As the class broke up, I chatted with another gray-haired woman named Mary who live a half a mile away. Mary had bought a new bike and was a little frightened of it, especially the multiple gear system. As we became acquainted, we learned that we knew many of the same people and had similar backgrounds. We became friends.

Our first adventure was on Sunday morning on the Beginner Women's Bike Ride, a ten-mile spin around the neighborhood. I wore an old red nylon jacket I had bought for ten dollars from an outlet catalog and some baggy nylon shorts. I clamped a twenty-year-old Styrofoam helmet onto my head. An old pair of Isotoner gloves left by my late mother-in-law completed my ensemble. My answer to padded shorts was a matted sheepskin seat cover.

The Neighborhood Bike Shop was at the bottom of a hill. I didn't know how to use the gears on the Browning to get me up the hill so I "paddled" until I gained enough momentum to get myself up onto the seat. The sheepskin seat cover stuck to my shorts and when I came to a stop, the crotch of my baggies caught on the front of the seat and the hem of my jacket caught on the back. The tension of riding in traffic wasn't relieved by my concern over my clothes. Marilyn, the leader, taught us how to get our pedals into position so we could make a smooth get away without paddling when the light changed. Each time I tried it, I banged my lower leg with the pedal. Each time it left a bruise. As I lurched from side to side, I realized that my beloved bike was way too tall for my five-foot frame. I perched on the seat and had to stretch to reach the pedals. Marilyn had us practice riding along the fog line at the side of a roadway and I wobbled with each stroke. Before we went up a gentle incline, Marilyn would holler, "Shift now." We practiced smooth turns, shifting down before stops and signaling. I fought my clothing at each stop. My hands began to ache at about four miles. Sweat caused my glasses to slip to down my nose. The last mile, before we came full circle to the Neighborhood Bike Store, involved going down Dead Man's Hill, a winding road through a golf course.

"Feather your brakes lightly," Marilyn said. "Keep your foot down on the outer curve and change positions as the road curves the other way."

I didn't understand why, but she had been right about everything so far, so I followed her instructions. It worked. I relaxed my death grip on the handlebars. My braking was feather-like. We went down the hill one at a time. Marilyn congratulated us on our courage in conquering an eighth of a mile gentle slope.

When I got home after a long stop for coffee and conversation, I coasted down the short hill to my garage, using feathery braking and shifted to a low gear so I could get up the hill again on my next outing. I immediately stripped off the sheepskin seat cover. My bottom was sore. My hands ached. A dull pain spread across my chest and shoulders. I examined the bruises on my calves where the pedals had whacked them. Under the nylon jacket my cotton t-shirt clung to my body like a wet towel. I couldn't work the release on the helmet and had to ask my husband to set me free. Despite my stiff walk and unquenchable thirst, I had had a wonderful time. I was hooked.

I am a thrifty and frugal person. Some call me a tightwad. A new bike was out of the question, but a different bike was a possibility. My eldest son is a Middle School shop teacher who specializes in bike repair. He scavenges for old parts and helps his students construct imaginative and innovative bikes.

"I'll get you a bike, Mom," he said.

A week later he showed up with the Frankenstein bike. The Frankenstein had started out as a 1980 Schwinn. The right shift lever was Shimano, the left some oddball brand from Costco. The brake levers, salvaged from a child's bike, fit my small hands perfectly. I replaced the hard arrow shaped racing saddle with a women's model. When I rode on it, I knew immediately that a man had designed it.

Mary and I set a goal to ride in the annual "Bridge Pedal," a community bike event held each August that takes cyclists across nine bridges, including two freeway spans over the Willamette River that runs through Portland, for a total of thirty eight miles.

A reexamination of equipment was in order. My first purchase was padded shorts. I bought a tube of Butt'r and smeared it liberally into the chamois and then on me as Patti had taught us. The chamois was much too wide for my physique and crunched up in folds forming hard ridges that rubbed the sensitive areas it was designed to protect.

A new helmet was mandatory. I added a mirror. Then a bell. Then a small satchel to attach to the carrier rack. I sacrificed sleekness for baggage room. New pedals with toe clips were next. I took the reflectors off the old Browning and installed them on Frankenstein. I bought a gray sweat-proof shirt on sale for eighteen dollars when I really wanted the one that said "Biker Chick" for sixty-five. For my birthday, my husband gave me a slim fitting water repellent jacket. I made myself a bright yellow vest from fabric on sale at JoAnn's, with pockets in the back, just like the real thing. I was beginning to look like a cyclist.

Mary and I started going out early on Sunday mornings when traffic was sparse. We loved exploring the city, crossing bridges we wouldn't dare to cross any other time. We enjoyed the chill, even the light fog, of winter mornings. I designed sheepskin "brake cozies," tubes the exact length of the brake levers and attached them to the cold metal with ponytail bands. We explored the industrial areas, checked out the construction of an aerial tram and biked along the Willamette River through the heart of the city.

As our stamina increased we added more miles. We only had a couple of months to get ready for the Bridge Pedal so we decided to try an organized ride with the Oregon Cyclists, the premier cycling club in the area. I contacted the leader and Mary and I set out to meet them at the appointed spot. Eight people were assembled, all dressed in the finest and most fashionable of cycle wear: the ubiquitous padded tights and shirts with designs of lightning bolts and flaming wheels across the chest. Mary and I joined two other women. One was tall and overweight with gray curls sticking out from under her helmet. Her broad beam hung out over the sides of the narrow saddle. In her electric yellow jacket, she was hard to miss.

There were no introductions, just a brief message from the leader, Les, who said that we would take a random route of his spontaneous choosing and would cruise at an average of fifteen miles an hour. We set out onto the streets of Northeast Portland, blowing though stop signs at will. I stuck to the rear because I feared my lack of experience riding in a group would get me in trouble, but I was not the last in line. The woman with gray curls was behind me. As we sped through the quiet streets, she fell further and further behind. Les and the other riders seemed unconcerned. After we turned a corner, I hesitated until a flash of yellow in my mirror told me she was still back there, three blocks behind.

We turned off the street behind a hedge to reach a pedestrian freeway overpass. The group sped on. I stopped and waited. "At least I'm not the slowest," I said to myself. "I'll be polite, even if no one else is. If that were me, I'd hate it."

Shortly after we crossed the overpass, which was thick with broken glass and assorted city debris, the leader called for a rest stop and we pulled into a pleasant neighborhood park. While the group milled around crunching energy bars and drinking from plastic bottles, Les approached me. He pushed a piece of paper with a name and phone number on it toward me and said: "I think you would fit in better with this other group." He took a gulp of water. "They are mostly around seventy and go a lot slower." I was dumbfounded. I watched to see if he did the same with the woman with gray curls when she finally showed up. He didn't.

I didn't think I was so bad. At least I was polite and considerate of the person who lagged three blocks behind. I could have kept up with the group if I hadn't waited for her. They never did reach fifteen miles per hour. After this incident I didn't try to keep up. The woman with gray curls fell behind, sometimes nearly out of sight. Les called for a coffee stop at a large inner city shopping mall. Most of the Oregon Cyclists didn't carry locks because of the extra weight so they asked Mary and me to lock their bikes to ours. They leaned the bikes, which did not have stands, against ours and we tethered as many together as our cables would reach. We entered the coffee shop looking like a tribe of aliens from outer space with our helmets, garish clothing and tight pants. I ordered coffee and a bagel and sat down with the group at a large table. No one spoke to Mary or me. We were the real aliens. Mary excused herself and headed for the restroom.

"Where's Marvin?" Les said.

"Oh, he's far back, as usual," someone in the group said. "I see his yellow jacket coming through the door now."

Marvin? Who was Marvin? The only person behind me was the woman with gray curls. Soon Marvin joined the group, coffee cup in hand. Mary returned to the table and sat next to me. She looked around and leaned over to whisper, "Wasn't there another woman?"

"It's Marvin," I said. "Marvin's the other woman."

We finished our coffee and set out refreshed. I stayed to the rear with Marvin far behind me. A handsome sixtyish man, who had hit on Mary unsuccessfully at the park, rode along beside me.

"I'm concerned about Marvin," I said. "He's always way behind,"

"Oh, he always brings up the rear," The man said. "He's the sweeper. He's been sweeping for us for years."

The Sweeper, and I had waited for him. Why didn't someone tell me? I had been waiting for the woman with gray curls who was left out of the pack because she was so slow.

Mary and I stepped up our routine without the Oregon Cyclists. I bought a computer, usually called a speedometer or odometer, to keep track of our workouts. Early one Sunday we went out to nearby town along the Columbia River and on our way back I announced that we were at thirty-seven miles.

"Let's go for forty," Mary said. "Across the bridge and back."

The Glen Jackson freeway bridge across the Columbia is two miles long with a bike path in the center. It slopes up from the Oregon side to the Washington side. I shifted into low as we went through a tunnel and came up in the center of the freeway. The noise from the traffic bounced against us in choppy waves. I breathed through my mouth so I couldn't smell the exhaust. My throat was raw. I wanted to close my eyes to protect them from the fumes. We rested briefly on the Washington side, drank some water and coasted back to Oregon. I struggled to keep an even course on the return trip so I wouldn't run into the cyclists lurching from side to side coming toward me as they pumped up the incline. My hands were paralyzed from gripping the handlebars as we passed forty miles with a cheer.

The next week we entered the Tour de Valley, a thirty-five mile excursion through the Willamette Valley with a spaghetti dinner for the finishers at the Oregon Garden. It took the two of us to get Mary's bike rack onto her car and the help of a neighbor to get the bikes up. The day was overcast but pleasant. We picked up our map, donned our neon chartreuse shirts with the logo of the sponsoring group, and set out. We were glad we couldn't go more than twenty miles an hour, because we would have missed the llamas and the cows that came to the fences to greet us in the lush farmland that marked the end of the Oregon Trail. An error in map reading extended our trip to forty-seven miles. I pushed Frankenstein up the last short hill. My thighs screamed with pain. A gentle rain fell as we entered the barn-like building where the smell of spaghetti sauce and sweat welcomed us. The dinner was free with registration, but water cost a dollar a bottle. I bought three.

As we were finishing up our pasta and salad, a tall white haired man with an ingratiating smile, like an aging game show host, approached our table. He looked right at me and said, "You must be Helen Cheek."

"I am," I replied, wondering how he knew me.

"You have won the award for being the oldest participant today," he said. "Congratulations."

That's how he knew me. He looked around for an old woman and found me. I was called up to the microphone, where he put his arm around me and presented me with the prize, a size extra large men's cycling shirt with the price tag of eighty bucks hanging from it, along with a pair of men's socks with red flames on the cuffs.

The day of the Bridge Pedal arrived, sunny and warm even at six in the morning. My son put our bikes in his pick-up and we arrived on the waterfront in good time for the six-thirty send off. I wore a new pair of shorts and a skintight yellow shirt. I convinced myself that one cannot ignore the importance of dressing a good game, especially if one is a mediocre player.

Promptly at six-thirty a gun went off somewhere. The pack was thick. Mary and I had attached large yellow bows to our helmets so we wouldn't lose track of each other. I was terrified of running into another cyclist and causing a crash. I practiced moving my head ever so slightly so I could sneak a look at my blind spot. Many of the cyclists were less skilled than I and I sensed danger all around. As we got under way, the crunch thinned out and I fell into my cadence, a biking term that means shifting gears so the spinning motion is consistent no matter what the speed or incline.

The third bridge was a freeway bridge with a long ascent. I regretted not outfitting Frankenstein with a granny gear. If it was called something else, maybe I would have, but I found it hard to ask for something called "granny." Sweating hard, we pulled up to the center of the bridge, and dismounted. There it was, the sight we had been working for a year to see. We could reach out and touch Mt. Hood. Neither of us spoke. We grinned at each other and hugged. A quick drink of water and we set out with renewed energy to conquer the rest of the bridges.

The familiar burning in my thighs asserted itself as the second freeway bridge soared in front of us. The gentle wind ruffled the bows on our helmets. We were in bikers' heaven as we posed for pictures at the summit, two five-foot senior ladies mugging for the camera. We cruised to the finish line exhausted and exhilarated at the same time. My searing muscles were elated.

Forgotten was the elitist attitude of the Oregon Cyclists. Gone was the condescending MC who presented me with a prize I couldn't possibly use. We rode home at a leisurely pace, enjoying the delicious pain of over-exertion, astonished at our accomplishment. I parked Frankenstein in the garage. If it had been a horse I would have given him a loving rubdown and patted his neck and said, "Nice going, Frank. Good boy. Good boy."

Pilgrim for Hire

Kristin Thiel

The news came via text message: U R FIRED. I called my brother, the usual culprit in such communications. When his voice-mail picked up, I hung up and connected to the internet. Within a minute I had an email from him, which contained nothing but a link to an article in the *Times*.

I tied back the curtain I'd hung from the ceiling to partition my studio and stepped from my office/bedroom into my kitchen/dining room/living room. There was a swallow of Riesling left in the fridge, and I carried the bottle back to my desk, finishing it off as I walked. I clicked to the article:

> VATICAN—The Roman Catholic Church announced today the formation of its new program Vatigrims, a version of the work currently performed by freelance pilgrims.

"Dammit, Danny!" I swore aloud at my absent brother as I punched my sister Trace's number into the phone.

"Focus on the real issue here," Trace said after I told her the news our brother had broken to me. "Danny didn't create the...these Vatigrims. Good God, what a name. Lola, tell Mr. Rohl I'll be just another minute. Pammy, I gotta go. Call me later, and we'll bounce around some ideas. Hugs and kisses."

> "The Pope and the Vatican saw the important need to help Catholics throughout the world accomplish such an important spiritual journey," said Vatican Spokesperson Michael Vasquez.
>
> Vasquez went on to say that the Church has never officially condoned the usage of freelance pilgrims, who have served 2.2 million Catholics worldwide since coming into existence in 1980, according to a 2005 poll conducted by

the Pew Charitable Trust. These "pilgrims for hire" walk for those who cannot themselves physically walk a pilgrimage. They started working on a local level, neighbors helping neighbors, but since the internet boom, many have established an international client base.

I want to stress to Catholics who have used a freelancer's services in the past that the Church is confident God heard their prayers and recognizes their effort put forth," Vasquez said. "But now that a Vatican-sponsored service is available, the Church—and God—assume that the faithful will use it."

I tugged down the Martin Luther caricatures calendar tacked to the wall behind my computer. Before I could even check my schedule, the phone rang.

"Oh, Pamela."

I heard Olivia O'Ryan's wavering voice on the other end of the line, in Chicago.

"Mrs. O'Ryan," I purred, flipping through the calendar pages. "I was just checking into fares for your pilgrimage. In July." Oh, God, checking into fares six months in advance? Was Olivia O'Ryan daft enough to buy my obvious lie and take pity on me?

"Oh, Pamela," Olivia O'Ryan repeated. "I was just listening to the radio."

"That's wonderful, Mrs. O'Ryan. You know my policy: I love when my clients give me a soundtrack for my journey. Just another way you really feel like you're the one walking."

God. That time, I meant the word. God. I'm talking to you. You. Geez.

"Pamela, dear, maybe you haven't heard, but there's a new service. *Sponsored by the Church*. It's wonderful news. I have to…."

"Mrs. O'Ryan, you've never expressed displeasure with my service…."

"Oh, no, no, no. I'm not displeased. I haven't ever been. But the Church… There are rules…."

"Surely they don't offer as much of a deal as I do." I tried appealing to her pocketbook.

"Actually, Pamela, it's miraculous."

I scrolled through the *Times* website as Olivia O'Ryan talked, and found the right sentence just as she began to rattle off the perks of hiring a Vatigrim.

This fee includes the pilgrim, matched with the client through a survey and interview process, and any room and board expenses he or she incurs; the buyer's prayer read at the end of the journey; the buyer's chosen hymns and Bible passages played from the support truck that follows the pilgrim; a certificate signed by local bishops along the route; two postcards or two letters, depending on the duration of the pilgrimage; additional letters for each sighting of the Virgin Mary, should there be any, and photos, if possible; a crucifix manufactured along the route; a vial of holy water; a certificate of completion signed by the Pope.

"By the Pope himself," Olivia O'Ryan sighed.

"Thank you for letting me know." I sighed, too, and drew a thick black line through the days I'd reserved for her.

"Some people can make a living doing marathons."

Trace had finally penciled in time to meet me, after my tenth voice mail message, when I could officially whine that all my clients had canceled appointments for that year and all future years. She offered her first suggestion, marathons, with her lips to a cocktail glass, the aquamarine-colored liquid halfway to her gaping mouth. She swallowed greedily.

I tapped my dropped jaw back into place and responded. "Doing a pilgrimage is not the same as doing a marathon. Trace, I appreciate you meeting me, but I really need some serious ideas here. I can't believe you think this is funny. *I have no job.*"

"Good God, Pamela. Don't tell me you've forgotten already? The six months I went without a *career*?" Her bright blue cocktail was nothing but a drop in the dimple where the stem attached to the glass. Trace wiggled her fingers in the air, calling to the server, while she admonished me.

"I. Have. No. Skills," I rephrased. "This is all I've done, Trace. You had other skills to fall back on. And even if you hadn't, there were other companies who did what you did when you were laid off. There are no other ways to be a pilgrim."

"Are Vatigrims not looking for recruits?"

God, it was frustrating when she ₀thought of something good, really great, before I did. I squeezed my napkin and gritted my teeth. Trace's eyebrows raised as she tipped back her new drink. She knew I knew…she knew she was right.

"If you're interested in being a Vatigrim, please submit an application online at w-w-w-dot…"

I hung up on the recorded voice. Okay, I could go to the Vatican's website and fill out an application, but Jesus Pete, they'd added the instructions to do so to their voice mail message. How many other Vatigrim hopefuls had called already?

Two months since the announcement, and everything had started to remind me of pilgrimages gone past, like the first sharp autumn day reminds one of school. Once something is gone, you can't seem to get it out of your head. Walking to the grocery store one day, a ghost pack hugged my shoulders, and I began counting my steps, setting the numbers to a tune I'd made up years before to help pass the time. At the store, I couldn't resist buying a chunk of cheese and a crusty loaf of bread, to taste the French countryside again, as though I were still on my way to Lourdes; the Jewish bagger appeared oh-so-Jewish—I swear he greeted me in Hebrew, a reminder of pilgrimages to Jerusalem.

How many shoes had I gone through over the years? How many frequent flier miles? How many lovers, who had wooed me with a hot meal, a warm bed, and accents, thick, like the chocolate—sweet, dark, bitter, depending on their region—they so often drizzled over me, licked off my skin with their warm, quivering tongues; who I had wooed by igniting their religious fervor?

Back at home, I gorged on the bread and cheese I'd bought, cracked open a bottle of wine. Collapsing drunk to my office/bedroom floor, I started sifting through my files. Some of the papers escaped and slithered under the curtain into the kitchen/dining room/living room. Thank God I hadn't input every client into my database; to feel the hard copies of their files made them a part of my life again. Olivia O'Ryan: Chicago, old, rich, one pilgrimage a year for her; Jean et Martinique d'Abo: Normandy, Jean too sick to travel; Pilar de Dios: Oaxaca, young, a mere babe but so devoted to her lord; she paid me by stealing coins here and there throughout the year from her maid's—her maid's!—purse. Clients from six of the seven continents and a scattering of the islands in between.

My ass was firm and round. My legs rippled with muscles. My skin held a year-round tan, and my eyes twinkled with health. I liked the faint wrinkles around them: from squinting into the sun. Trace, who sat at a computer most of her days, looked like a porcelain doll.

My phone rang, and I stared at it, enjoying its chirp and the pulse of its red light. I counted to thirty after it stopped ringing—the numbers sliding once again into that walking ditty I had composed—and picked up the receiver. I had a message.

"Hi, this message is for Pamela. This is Tanisha Rollins. I'm a fellow freelancer. We met about two years ago? In Spain? The Santiago de Compostela? I kept your card. I just wondered, how were you doing? We only live about an hour apart, and I'm home a lot these days. If you want to grab a drink or lunch or something sometime. Well, I'd appreciate it."

I scribbled Tanisha Rollins's phone number on the back of little Pilar's contact sheet and called her back immediately. Her high-pitched laughter when she heard my voice crumbled into a cough. We made plans for happy hour.

Tanisha introduced herself to me with a skinny cigarette dangling from her lips. The evening passed, and I never saw her without one in her mouth.

"I actually did fill one out," Tanisha said about the Vatigrim application, her eggplant-colored nails tapping through a dish of mixed nuts and olives.

"Really?"

"Yep."

"And?"

Tanisha's gray-blue eyes were like hazy pools, reflecting me back at me. "Now, what do you think?"

"Well, see, that's exactly why I didn't even bother!"

"You gotta try," Tanisha coughed again, this one grinding into a laugh. "'Cause if you don't, you know, you end up with no clients."

"Which is so different from you," I said with a snap of my head, feeling confident with this stranger, downing my third beer.

"Which is so different from me!" Tanisha's laughter continued.

I joined her, and then the beer I'd drunk started to turn and hit me differently. "What are we going to do?" I asked without laughter. Tanisha coughed quietly. I folded my arms across the table and slowly, as what felt like hours ticked by without an answer from Tanisha, I laid my head on top of them.

When I got into the pilgrim-for-hire business, there were two kinds of people involved: swindlers and the deeply religious. I was among the first who joined to see the world: we escapees from hometowns all over the planet. Trace went abroad during college, and my brother, Danny…I really didn't know what Danny is or was. But I was sure he had been involved in schemes abroad. About to graduate from high school with neither the grades for higher education nor the interest in clerical or technical work, I spent a lot of time slouching around the school's career center.

Freelancing as a pilgrim was actually listed in the tattered copy of an "alternatives to the Peace Corps" booklet I found there. In the blunt words of the authors of the guide, a free-lovin' spirit like myself could easily bump a nun-in-training out of position and set up a business. People who hired pilgrims didn't necessarily want a church mouse grabbing for her own holy crumbs; they wanted people interested in the world and confident enough to travel solo in it. The pilgrimage had to succeed for the buyers to get their just reward, and it was more likely to go well with someone…why, golly, Sister Mary Margaret, with someone like me.

Religion was never a motivating force for me, though I did come to respectfully say that I was "serving" my clients. They had this intense goal that I couldn't help but admire on some level, maybe because I'd never felt such intensity myself.

I met Tanisha again. Her hair was longer, swirling past her shoulders, and she'd changed her nail color to a blue that matched her eyes. The whole package scared me. She looked like a cool storm brewing.

"We're going to fight them," she told me, her side of the table clear and clean, with her hands folded over it, and mine cluttered with the bottle I'd finished while waiting for her, the bottle I was halfway through, and a plate of gooey nachos I'd hoped she'd help me with.

I snorted. "The Vatigrims? I don't think so."

"Pamela, don't be a fool," Tanisha hissed. "This control they have won't last. You can't control a whole group of people. We'll undercut them. People lead with their wallets."

"What about the extras? The holy water?"

Tanisha spit on the table. "There's your holy water."

I had an ass like a melon and the humility of a servant, and at some point not long ago, men had whispered to me in a bouquet of languages. I pushed back my chair and walked. It was the first time in two decades that I'd started walking without a destination in mind.

There was a church on the corner. There was always a church on the corner. It had been years since I'd been inside one without someone paying me. When I read in the entryway that confession was in session, I walked straight to the traditional wooden booths along the far wall. The first one had a green light, and I stepped inside; kneeled. As I spoke, I rested my fingertips on the wooden lattice that separated the priest from me. I wished I could physically feel the forgiveness, just as I felt the wood. I was sorry that I'd ever gotten into this business, and I was sorry for drinking too much lately.

When I began wondering if those were really sins worthy of confession, I began confessing Tanisha's plans; I even coughed a little, just like her. That led to confessing for Danny, the only other person in my life who scared me. For as long as I'd known him, he'd been all fists and deals. His jaw cracked when he talked, from being punched so often; the scabbed cracks across his knuckles, from hitting back, never had time to heal. I didn't know what exactly he'd been up to lately, but I could guess. So for him I just said, my voice deepening, "Forgive me, Father, for I have made poor decisions for more than forty years."

It was easy; it was calming. As when I worked as a pilgrim, I felt an escape. Taking someone else's sins and releasing them…for money. I made the sign of the cross hastily as I backed out of the confessional. A middle-aged woman in a tweed suit—on her lunch break, probably—shifting her weight and playing her pearls like a rosary, stepped forward, seemingly to take my space in the confessional. I didn't move out of her way but instead extended my hand.

"Excuse me for saying so, but you look a little nervous to confess." I held her hand, as if drawing from her the proper voice and emotion to use to convey her sins. "I know how imhportant this is to you. May I help?"

The Weight of Loss

Lori Maliszewski

Recently I've found myself obsessed with women's butts. I look at their nice round derrières with longing, and wonder if they can feel their sit bones like I can when I sit on a hard surface. I wonder if they love and appreciate the beauty and proportion of their backsides, or despise their asses like I used to despise mine before the cancer. Before my body weight oozed off, pound by pound.

Most of the time it's a slow drip, but sometimes it's a gush and it feels like it won't stop. *This is it,* I think. This is the time I've dreaded, when the outward manifestation of the disease takes over. When I can't hide it anymore.

Loss is the axis upon which cancer spins its destruction. It consumes your soft tissue—your self-worth, faith, health, heart, vigor, dreams, trust—until all that's left are the bones of your former self. Loss becomes the norm and you search for yourself in the hard angles of what remains.

For most of my adult life, I've been well within a normal weight range—slender but always wanting to be just a little bit thinner, not much, just a pound or two. *Be careful what you wish for.* These days I eat constantly, even when I'm full and it hurts, but to no avail. Paul Simon described me perfectly: *slip sliding away.*

For as long as I can remember, I'd regularly hold up a hand mirror to check out my butt in the bathroom mirror. For years I lamented about its size concluding to others, "I've got great child-bearing hips." A lot of good that did me. No kids after years of trying. Now all I see in the mirror is my tiny sagging ass and I mourn the loss. Finally I had to stop looking. It's ridiculous to grieve the loss of something you've always hated.

For months, I stubbornly wore pants so baggy it looked like I was wearing someone else's clothes. I swore to everyone that I'd fatten up and they'd fit again.

It helped when I finally admitted to myself that I might not gain the weight back, and that I should buy pants that fit. My friend Souzie, whose lovely butt is round and full and whose favorite sport is shopping, cajoled me into a store and had me outfitted in two new pairs of pants before I could think twice about it. What a difference it made to have pants that fit. It wasn't my ass that was sagging, but my old jeans. Still my backside remained un-impressive and was not the abundant twin mounds that used to spill out of my husband's hands. To me, my body has become a disappointing drought of flesh.

Before I lost all this weight, I'd tell my friend, Michelle, that I had a nice pear-shaped figure. She'd roll her eyes with disgust. "You're not pear-shaped. You're shaped like a ruler." She'd roll her eyes again as if she couldn't believe what a complete idiot I was. Then to make her point perfectly clear, she'd rip a piece of paper from her pad, grab a pen and draw a pear and a straight line. "This is you." She jabbed her pen at the straight line. "And this is me." She drew several heavy-handed circles around the pear. Michelle has a charming fanny, but of course doesn't think so, and has offered to donate a portion of it to me. I'd happily take whatever body fat she's willing to part with, but I'm certain her husband wouldn't want to lose an ounce of her.

The butt I currently admire most is that of my yoga teacher. Bev's is a perfect heart-shaped version—the kind that men look at not once but twice, their eyes dripping with lust. And at 55 she doesn't have youth on her side. She moves with such fluidity demonstrating the yoga asanas —her buttocks sway beneath her tights like a gently rolling ocean. It gives her a center of gravity that provides balance, grace and stability.

Maybe that's why I bemoan all my angles and bones and miss having an ample butt so much. I feel so wobbly and ungrounded, like I don't carry enough weight to stay connected to the earth. I worry that should the loss continue, gravity might decide not to bother with me anymore and toss me away to the firmament.

Dummies

Tiel Aisha Ansari

You call them "dummies,"—mannequins with wooden
faces and plastic hearts—they know more than you think.
One day they will break your plate-glass windows and march
with their feather boas and wool cloches
above nude shining torsos bent at impossible angles—
unliving, undead and not to be trifled with.
Not-real women, not-real bodies inside not-real clothes
marked For Display Only. Arm in arm they'll shout
shattering windows, glass prisons
crushed to sparkling sugar
by the unbleeding feet of the vanguard crossing against lights
tearing awnings to ragged banners. Not to wear,
and not because they don't know they're naked—
that's how they were made after all. But these women
are done with rags, done with glass houses, done with
selling selling selling being sold
standing still being stared at being ignored
being on display being merchandise being backdrops for merchandise.
They're on the move. They've left the background. They own
themselves.

Skeleton Dance

Tiel Aisha Ansari

So it's a waltz? I'll let you lead, my friend.
We're just wasting time waiting for the end.
Icicle bones move under the snowman's skin
with glacier patience. They say time mends
but also wears the fabric of the world thin.
Give this ancient globe a brand new spin—
it'll fly apart. Don't cry over oceans spilled
like milk; that's how the Milky Way begins.

I tell you only what you know. Time kills.
Seeds wait in old dry lakes for rain to fill
the expectations of a bygone age. Your bones
are ivory and ice, long dry, but still
tatters of skin hang from your fleshless fingers.
A skeleton dancing while daylight lingers.

Condemnation

Rachael Cate

I was only a woman
when the bells began to ring.
When they shuffled me along
with lame feet,
I shrank to half a man.
When they placed me in the rain,
many cold hands fumbling under an artificial white—
When they locked me in the corner,
I cried small tears
& smaller
from eyes that betrayed a mind defined,
exposed, revealed, erased,
scattering quickly like scurrying roaches
suddenly under unrelenting lights.

Show me myself,
like a mean bulb
upon a secret weakness.
Tell me myself,
Your wayward child.
Somewhere in the back of my small space
that is no space,
I see the *word*, etched above my soul:
criminal.
like hands or eyes of hatred.

I looked for your eyes, then,
saw them searching in the distance, so very far away.

After my condemnation—
public, naked, and unknown—
the shell of me receding like a crumpled candy wrapper:
I've come to meet my other half.
The nowhere-in-the-mirror me
that loves, and prays, and knows.
I give her ears and eyes and lips;
somewhere out of *me*, she grows.

Some Hair Makes the Girl

Melanie Springer Mock

I am a girl.

No one seems to know this, except for my family (and sometimes I think they wonder).

In a public restroom, I am confronted by well-meaning old ladies with cotton candy hair who tell me this is the women's room, perhaps I could not read the sign? As if, at age twelve, I cannot read the sign "women's" on the door, or wonder why there are so many ladies in a bathroom meant for men.

Sometimes, in public restrooms, I am confronted by mean girls, feather-haired teenagers who assume I am in the women's room because I am a twelve-year-old pervert seeking titillation: a peek at the stalls, the tampon box, or at an adolescent peeing. They do not kindly misdirect me. They say "Get out." (I leave. I linger by the door until the girls pass by, glaring, then slip into the restroom again.)

But I am a girl.

No one seems to know this because my short afro hair won't grow straight and smooth like everyone else's. It must be short and fluffy, like a Q-tip, or (in seventh grade) like Dr. J, or (in tenth grade) like Michael Jackson. When I tie a bow to a curl it gets buried. When I try using a barrette it slides off. I use water to part and flatten my hair, but thirty minutes later, when it dries, I look like James Brown, three puffs on my head with a barely distinguishable crease.

My mother does not encourage me to wear feminine clothes. These cost more money. We do not have more money. I wear my brother's old clothes, his Tough Skins and t-shirts. Or my best friend's hand-me-down western wear, gingham shirts with pearly buttons, leather belt with horse patterns, platter-sized silver buckle.

I am a Q-tip headed cowboy who is really a girl.

I decide my name should be Terry, so people who think I am a boy will not be embarrassed, or confused, when I say "My name is Melanie."

In third grade, we moved to a new town. At recess, my first day of school, I hear the murmurs of discontented kids wanting to know if I am a boy or a girl. Not even Sheryl, the special friend assigned for the day sets them straight. Finally, someone asks me. When I admit I am a girl, the boys descend, tripping me, throwing rocks, betrayed because I am not the boy they hoped would play with them, nor (really) the girl with whom they could fall in love.

With the advent of puberty, I become a Dr. J-headed, flat-chested boy who is really a girl. My friends grow ample breasts, buy big bras, become women. My mom buys me a training bra because it's time. I am appalled by the bra's construction, the crisscrossed front apparently meant to lift and separate 32AAA air. I rip off the delicate cloth flower on its front, because it seems too feminine underneath my camp t-shirt: a stupid fabric flower where no one will see it. Strangers must be confused by the bra-wearing boy.

In ninth grade, we moved again. In P.E. class, the first day of school, I hear the sneers of malcontents, wanting to know whether I am a boy or a girl. I sit on the bottom bleacher, hunched over hard so that the girls laughing behind me can see my bra straps, can know I am a girl. Apparently, they cannot see the straps through my heavy t-shirt. Finally someone asks me what I am. The P.E. teacher doesn't hear the answer, and he tells me to come along with the boys to get my locker assignment. When I tell him my name, he apologizes, and sends me back to the laughing girls. My face burns.

At my new high school I look like a Michael Jackson-headed boy trying hard to be a girl. Mom buys me clothes at the Salvation Army. I wear big earrings, vinyl-heeled shoes, pastel pink knitted vests. I go to the prom with my best friend, who sees past my masculine, puffy hair (so I think; he comes out as a gay man ten years later). My friends are pretty, and have boyfriends and sex. By association, I also feel pretty, and anticipate I will soon have my own good fornication.

But then, my senior year, I am at the state fair with my most beautiful, most sexy friend. I am wearing big earrings, and feeling pretty. Two cute but drunk boys come up to us, and tell my friend that she is dating the ugliest guy they have ever seen, that she should drop me and hang out with them. She laughs and blows them off, and we continue down the midway. I am embarrassed and want to go home.

A year later, I move away to college. Michael Jackson, before his creepy feels in Neverland, remains my hairstyle inspiration. Still, on the first day of class, I hear boys behind me wondering whether I am one of them, or not. In the first semester, I nearly get kicked off a girls' dorm floor because it is not open hours when boys can visit. In the first year, I am set up on a blind date, with a young man who subsequently turns me down when he sees me, suddenly remembering a big test for which he is unprepared.

Enough. I try growing my hair long. The advent of miracle hair products straightens the Q-tip, Dr. J., Michael Jackson 'fros. Without the mousse and gels and creams, my hair is big and wild and puffy, like Medusa—or Diana Ross, after a ride in her LeBaron Convertible. With my "product" (as the beautician calls it), my hair is long with perfectly cork-screwed curls, the envy of my peers.

I meet a mullet-wearing man who likes me. He says he finds me sexy. He likes my long and coiled product-laden hair. We date and fall in love. He meets another woman with naturally wavy hair and a cool name, Petra, and we break up. I go on a blind date with a man who, when he sees me, has no big tests for which he is unprepared. He finds me sexy, and likes my hair. His name is John Candy—not the fat John Candy, but this one is bald and likes ham radio. (We do not date, do not fall in love.)

Finally, I am recognized for what I am: a female. Mulleted men and bald men, furry-backed men, and combed-over men. They like my hair and find me attractive. I walk into public restrooms with impunity. I wear bras with little flowers, and barrettes and bows. I become confident in my sexuality.

So confident, that when I grow tired of product and barrettes and bows, I decide to cut off my long hair. Become like Annie Lennox or Halle Berry, when they had short hair: confident, sexy, short-haired women. On the first day at my new job, teaching seventh grade boys in a reformed school, I hear the same sniggering. The same questions: Is she? Or is she a he? Finally, one of the boys asks. The next day, I purchase the biggest earrings I can find, and hope for the best.

Boyish

AnnCary

Y ou remember the buzzing of those obnoxious fluorescent lights in the waiting room of the hospital. You were six and they were going to take your tonsils out. You were scared and nervous, so much so that you didn't notice them calling you "Dan." Years later your mother would tell you and laugh about it. You'd laugh too, but not because it was funny.

When your family went to Lake Okoboji every summer for vacation, you went fishing with your brother instead of lying on the beach with your sister. Your dad gave you his old tackle box and took you to Scheel's Sporting Goods to pick out fake purple worms that reminded you of gummy worms.

When you're at your grandparents one summer the men of the family plan a fishing trip for the day. They don't invite you, and you wonder if it's because you're a girl or because you're little and don't have your left-handed Snoopy fishing pole. When you ask to go along they hum-haw for a while but eventually say okay. You go upstairs to change into your Air-Jordan tank top and shorts, and when you get back down all the women are getting ready to go window shopping downtown. You run outside to catch up with the guys. But you feel like they don't want you to come, like you don't belong, so you decide not to go. You tell them you'll go with the girls, and then make sure the girls think you've gone with the guys. When they've both left you head back in to the big old farm house, all alone. You start to cry, partly because you're scared but more because you're alone and don't want to be. You hide under the bench of the organ until they come back and find you there, crouched in a ball and still crying.

They don't allow you to wear earrings when you play soccer, and you don't yet have boobs in sixth grade, so in that gold and black uniform people sometimes think you're a boy. At Red Robin one day after a game you hold the door for an older man with a cane. He says, "Thank you, sir," and you turn your eyes to the ground, glad none of your teammates or their parents heard. As you sit at lunch the only thing you're able to swallow are the tears you're holding back. In the safety of your mom's Aerostar minivan you tell her what happened in between sobs. She doesn't know what to say to comfort you, suggests you try and grow your hair out. You agree, even though you really like it short.

For years, through middle school and high school, you keep your hair long. Your hairdresser-mother seems pleased, especially when your thick shiny hair falls down past your shoulders in your senior pictures. But the same ponytail that bounces around the soccer field does not fly so well at church, especially when it's wet. You are told not to arrive at church with wet hair ever again. Since you're allowed to forgo skirts and dresses and wear pants and polos on non-holidays, you figure you can do your family this one small favor. During a post-church trip to the mall you mention it would be fun to get a neck tie, that you think it would be sexy when you dress up. Your mother looks disgusted, like someone who's realized they just ate raw chicken. You don't mention it again.

Your first year of college you cut your hair off, an act that feels defiantly freeing. Your mother cuts it for you, even though you know she doesn't want to. To balance your boyishness you wear pink, lots of pink. Your mother buys you a pink leather purse. The leather is the softest you've ever felt and it closes with this convenient little magnet, two features that make you want to carry it everywhere. Your friends make fun of your pink purse; get many a good laugh out of it. You just sit quietly with a coy smirk though, knowing why you really wear it. It's the ultimate "fuck you" to anyone who thinks life is black and white, that boyish girls can't be girly.

You get ballsy after college and decide one week that you need to move to Portland. You give two weeks notice at the restaurant, buy an Amtrak ticket, pack two suitcases, book a room at the youth hostel on Hawthorne for your first week, and kiss Iowa goodbye. In the hostel you meet overbearing, too-old-to-still-be-staying-in-hostels Ruth, who likes to make everyone's business her own. She looks you up and down as you return from a stroll on Hawthorne, takes in your khakis, gray Puma sneakers, signature pink purse, and says, "Well, aren't you an enigma." Later that day when you finally get the chance to look up the word "enigma," this pisses you off. For the rest of your stay in the hostel you wear as much pink as you can, just to keep Ruth guessing.

After a year in Portland you're still attempting to be the adult you're not yet ready to be. Standing in Safeway after work one night you're looking at the smoked salmon. A clerk notices your contemplation and asks if she can help you. She calls you sir. When you turn to face her to say no, you smile to ease her embarrassment, unsuccessfully. As you're driving home you realize it doesn't hurt anymore, didn't feel at all how it did when you were a little girl. You wonder if it doesn't hurt because you truly don't care or if you went numb because the pain became too much.

That winter you and your girlfriend Kelly head up to the mountains with a couple of friends for a weekend of cross-country skiing. Sitting in the log cabin Kelly comments on how hot your new jeans are, your vintage 501 Levis that, unlike all your women's pants, don't reveal your ass and crack. You revel in the fact that you finally had the guts to go into stores and try on enough men's pants to figure out your size and preferred cut. When you express how much you *really* like men's pants, Teresa says, "Well, you're kind of like a guy, a gay guy." You don't know what to say. You're not angry so much as caught off-guard. Gillian shoots her a "that was not appropriate and totally not pan-gender conscious" look and the conversation goes elsewhere. The next morning you think back on her comment and decide it was quite justified. You eat like a boy. Have the libido of a boy. You're athletic. Analytical. Fastidious. Tidy. Meticulous about your car. The one perplexing flaw however, if you are truly like a gay guy, is that you like girls. You slough off the comment and realize that again, you didn't feel that familiar pain of your childhood.

For your twenty-third birthday you buy yourself a pink neck tie. You buy it at a vintage store for five dollars and know it is the coolest thing you own. You excitedly show it to Kelly and when she says, "Try it on!" you realize you don't know how. Neither does she. Sheepishly you walk to your bedroom mirror, assuming you won't be able to figure it out. But for some reason, it's the most natural thing you've ever done. You smile as you realize you tied it perfectly on the first try. You think it's fate, a sign that you were destined to wear ties. You fold down your collar and tuck in your fitted shirt, the one that makes your boobs look really big. When you look in the mirror and smile that boyish grin—feeling amazingly sexy and feminine—you know what you didn't even a short while ago. It just doesn't hurt anymore.

The Bösendorfer

Alida Thacher

It takes five years to create each Bösendorfer Grand Piano. It takes a lifetime to hear all that yours has come to tell you.

The beauty of my Bösendorfer overwhelmed me: cased in walnut with inlaid gold; massive elegantly shaped legs, brass pedals, a hand-carved music rack. It was strung with lower tensile wire, and its bass strings were made of iron, as they were in the nineteenth century. The ivory keys were yellowed with a century of musicians' fingertips. The delicacy of its details was a counterpoint to its immensity. Seven feet long and five feet wide, it sprawled grandly across my living room floor like a small airplane.

When Franz Liszt gave concerts, he would pound into the notes so forcefully that it was not uncommon for him to break the strings of three or four pianos each night. Several extra instruments were kept offstage as replacements. Finally they built him a Bösendorfer.

The exquisite simple beauty of the overtones in a single note can move the soul to tears.

And recognizing that I have to get rid of mine also moves my soul to tears.

My great uncle Samuel gave it to me. He was a concert pianist, the toast of Europe during the teens and twenties. From Boston, he studied at the New England Conservatory of Music, mentored by Arnold Schönberg and Eric Satie. He never married. The Archduchess Gisela of Austria presented him with his Bösendorfer after attending a series of Beethoven sonatas that she believed were responsible for the birth of her long prayed-for son.

My mother was his favored niece. She was also a musical prodigy, mastering the cello by the age of six to play "Claire de Lune" to a spellbound group of judges at the Röthenberg Festival. They awarded her the Plume D'Or, despite the fierce competition from ten adults who had over 150 years of concert performance experience between them.

It is love that makes me do it, of course: love and devotion and commitment.

Buoyed by their success at Mother's Plume D'Or, my great uncle and grandparents ratcheted up her career path. She was sent to a private school half-days; the other half of her days were spent practicing her cello, being coached in theater and choreography, and performing. Uncle Samuel frequently flew in from Budapest or Tokyo or Cairo to practice with her. She was forced to wear long ringlets and short skirts and anklets with little white flats well past sixth grade. In other words, she began that age-old anti-feminist tradition of lying about her age sometime around her seventh year. The theory was that she would compete much better the younger she appeared. She was an outcast with her peers, treated like a freak, laughed at and teased. But it wasn't until she was twelve, when she shot up to 5 foot 6 inches, and the extreme self-consciousness of puberty began to smother her like a blanket, that she started to deeply resent her family.

The Bösendorfer factory owns a forest outside of Vienna. It is the job of one man to go out and knock on trees to hear which one should become the next piano. When the right one is chosen, it is felled, and then it cures outside for several years. Living through the seasons, the rains and harsh sunshine and winds and snows, it becomes wise enough to be a Bösendorfer.

In her first year of high school, my mother snapped. She refused to touch her instrument, insisted on public school, and lived out four very rebellious years. Then she went on to college, majored in accounting, and married my father, who was working on his MBA. Uncle Samuel threatened to disown her, but then I arrived.

When I was born, Uncle Samuel gave us a baby grand for a christening gift. By this time, my mother had become rather sentimental about music education (although not her own), and she saw that our household was filled with classical recordings during waking and sleeping hours. I loved it. My first word was "forte"; my earliest memory was throwing up at Handel's Messiah.

After the wood for the Bösendorfer has seasoned, each Bösendorfer is hand-crafted, a process that takes 68 weeks. It's said that each instrument picks up personality traits and emotions of those who work on her. If a technician is angry—if his wife has left him or he has quarreled with a friend—the action on the piano he works on will be too hard. If he is sad or insecure, she will hit too soft.

My mother began to formally teach me piano at the age of two and a half. She would lift me onto the piano seat, cover my hands with her hands, and guide me through scales and chords, simple melodies and bass lines. By the time I was four, I was sight-reading, and by the time I was six, I could play all of Chopin's Mazurkas with my eyes closed. At nine, I got my first invitation to solo with the symphony.

At my mother's insistence I went to public school every day, but I spent the time between school and dinner at the conservatory as part of the young musicians program, studying under every maestro. I usually spent an hour on homework each evening, but after that, I practiced several hours more before my father sent me off to bed. Uncle Samuel would arrange performances for me several times a year, usually scheduled during school vacations. He would meet me in some faraway city like Amsterdam or San Francisco, and we together would dazzle our audiences with Beethoven and Rachmaninoff and Bach.

The sanders working on the Bösendorfer hang pictures of naked women on the walls of their work area. They claim this is so when they work the piano, she will feel like the flesh of a woman's body.

This was my life through high school, and then upon graduation I entered the conservatory full time, where I remain today. Great Uncle Samuel was delighted with my passion for the piano and supported me entirely. He began by funding my lessons, then the tuition for the young musicians program, and then he paid for all living and schooling expenses when I became a full-time conservatory student. He rarely missed a recital or concert of mine.

I think he never got over his heartbreak from my mother's rejection of the cello, and never quite trusted her influence over me, so when I turned twenty-one, and he was well into his eighties, he flew into town to find me respectable living quarters. Time to cut the apron strings, he told me. He worried that if he wasn't there to help me, I might never leave my parents' home. He took me from one flat to the next around town, clearly driven by some kind of inner vision, and when he found it, he knew immediately. It was a sunny two bedroom on the second floor. It had an enormous living room, with a wide balcony overlooking the park. It was acoustically perfect. The walls, ceiling and floor were soundproof; there was never any indication that anyone else lived in the building except for occasional sightings at the mailboxes. Don't worry about furniture, he told me. I'll take care of that.

So in a couple of weeks after the sale closed, furniture trucks arrived with a long couch and a couple of leather arm chairs and a velvet chaise lounge, a bureau, and a queen-sized bed. In another delivery truck came elaborate kitchen furnishings and boxes and boxes of musical scores.

But the biggest surprise came in the final truck. It became abundantly clear why Uncle Samuel was only satisfied by a place with a living room the size of a ballroom and wide double doors to the balcony. He had sent his beloved Bösendorfer, along with a crew of men who had to remove the outside doors and hoist the massive piano up over the balcony and through the entry.

The Bösendorfer is known for her warm clear sound, as well as her power, both fluid and suggestive. Those who own a Bösendorfer swear she is alive, that she understands those who play it, for better or worse. She speaks, and she listens to you. She understands your feelings, and reflects them back to you like a mirror of acoustics. She forms with her musician an unbreakable bond.

Uncle Samuel died shortly after my Bösendorfer arrived, able to let go knowing it was both safe and adored.

My life was very sweet those days. I had begun teaching and was happy giving lessons, taking classes and playing recitals. I couldn't learn enough about music history and theory. I felt content to spend the rest of my life at the conservatory, and thanks to Uncle Samuel's stipend, I could afford it.

My days consisted of rising around eight, eating a bowl of oatmeal, practicing on the Bösendorfer for an hour, then catching the 9:40 bus to school. I took classes and gave lessons until 5:30, then took the 5:45 back to my flat. On weekends, when I wasn't performing, I would spend most hours practicing, except for Sunday night dinners at my parents.

I met Sarah shortly afterwards, a complete surprise to me, although she told me later she had been planning it. She took the 9:40 bus to her job at the mall—she sold shoes—and since she got on at an earlier stop and got off after I did, she was able to observe me through my entire ride. I was oblivious, as I was about most of what went on around me. One day, as I was studying Ravel's Gaspard de la Nuit, an exceedingly complicated score, she sat in the empty seat next to me and offered me some peanuts. I looked up, startled, and found myself staring into her large sea green eyes, at her plump pink lips and her thick smooth black hair that reached down her back. Her beauty shocked me.

She began asking me about the music I was reading and what the conservatory was like and what instrument I played. I am generally very quiet, but I found it easy to talk to her from the moment I met her. She started saving a seat for me, and after about a week, she held my hand as we rode. (I would have been much too shy to take her hand first!) We began to meet for coffee. At the end of the day, she came to the conservatory, and we walked to the local café frequented by music students. There she told me the story of her life.

When she was a baby, her father died in the war—the silly one, she said, although she thought all wars were silly. Her mother never formed another long attachment, and Sarah remained an only child. They moved frequently, her mother dabbling in climates: the steamy languor of Louisiana, the deep snows, lush summers, and brilliant autumns of northern Michigan, the soggy winters of the Pacific Northwest, the dry sunny heat of the Nevada desert.

They had moved here two years ago, just in time for Sarah's high school graduation. At that point, she decided to jump off the moving train of her mother's momentum, answered a roommate wanted ad, and relocated into a wild household of four men and two women who never seemed to sleep or clean. She did have her own room, a tiny thing between the living room and the only bathroom.

She had held a series of jobs since then: a receptionist for a law firm (she couldn't afford the clothes), a waitress at a German restaurant (she experienced paralyzing stage fright when required to sing "Happy Birthday" with the accordionist), an oil jockey with Jiffy Lube (she couldn't do it in under 10 minutes). She had been selling shoes at Florsheim's for the last six months, and she liked the quiet carpeted floors and the soft padding of stockinged feet.

Every day I was more entranced. I had problems concentrating on my work. My mind wandered, imagining whom Sarah was fitting for shoes or thinking about the cobalt blue sweater she wore yesterday. I was falling in love quickly and didn't quite know what to do. I invited her to my flat for dinner. We decided on Saturday, since neither of us had to work the next day. I was nervous, of course, and spent the day cleaning and making eggplant parmesan and playing romantic sonatas on the Bösendorfer.

When she arrived, a little late, she was visibly overwhelmed by my flat. I was overwhelmed by her scent, her form-fitting red dress, and her hair swept atop her head, exposing that long graceful neckline. Of course she would notice my Bösendorfer first. She had never seen a grand piano except on television, certainly never the enormous Bösendorfer. She asked me to play something for her. I was glad, since I was almost faint from nerves and emotion, and the Bösendorfer was the only thing that could focus me.

I warmed up with a Bach fugue, then moved on to a lovely Chopin waltz. Next, I began Beethoven's Opus 110, but I was only in the second movement when she put her arms around my neck and whispered in my ear, asking if I knew any Celine Dion. She had met her in line at the Las Vegas Safeway and said she was the nicest person in the world.

When I told her unhappily that Celine Dion was not in my repertoire, she kissed me deeply, and pulled me into the bedroom.

I had never been with a woman before, but I had a lifetime of experience exploring the tones, power, and sensuality of a finely tuned instrument. Her skin was like smooth mahogany, and her responses to my caresses were immediate but varied, depending on how hard or soft I stroked her, whether I caressed her navel or bottom. When I took her breast in my mouth, I suddenly understood why men played the trumpet. Although I would have been content to explore the nooks and crannies of her body for hours, she wanted *poco più allegro*. She guided my head between her legs, and I played her like a piccolo, *staccato non troppo*. Her body arpeggioed. Then I penetrated her, *forte*, then *pianissimo*, then *forte, forte, forte, crescendo, fortissimo!* And our arpeggios shook the bed and our voices sang out and I thanked Uncle Samuel for the flat's great acoustics.

That night I got up, naked, and pounded out some Beethoven, then Shostakovich, then Tchaikovsky. The Bösendorfer sparkled with my joy. I was tired and somewhat sore and had never felt so alive in my life.

We made love again in the early morning, *pianissimo, dolce*. I kissed her eyelashes and her forehead and her ears and drifted off to sleep.

I couldn't get enough of Sarah, her smell like lavender and ylang ylang, her taste like popcorn and marshmallows. I loved her voice. She spoke in a melodic drawl, low and sexy like an oboe snaking through the grass, and her laughter chimed like a carillon. Every time I caught sight of her—buttoning her blouse, opening the refrigerator, brushing her teeth—the intensity of my desire almost hurt.

She moved in soon after. We were spending every night together anyway. She brought over a few possessions: an Indian bedspread, a crock-pot, a small television set. Her dresses fit easily in my closet—I'd never been much on clothes.

I stopped playing the Bösendorfer in the evenings, since the noise bothered her, and besides, she told me, she was jealous of my time. Instead we huddled under the blankets and watched "American Idol" and "Nanny 911."

When I woke early, I would quietly close the door and tiptoe to the piano, playing soft chords and scales and bass lines. But if Sarah woke, I would feel her stare from the doorway, arms crossed, before she would urge me back to bed.

After awhile, Sarah stopped going to work. When I worried about it, she told me not to, that it was a lousy job. Every evening it seemed I came home from the conservatory to surprises—her black underwear strewn across the dining room floor, a jar of Cheez Whiz open on the counter, chairs pushed oddly around the living room floor.

She frequently begged me to stay home with her, and for the first time in my life, I began to skip my lessons. We would spend much of the day making love, then we would walk through the park or shop for groceries or stroll through neighborhoods looking at houses we would someday buy. She didn't let me near the piano—those days, she said, were all hers; she wasn't sharing.

I began to miss my Bösendorfer exceedingly, to crave her. When I walked through the door, I would run my hand across her sleek shiny top. I would sit on the bench to talk to Sarah about her day, although she would soon take my hands and pull me to the couch. I found I could never play my piano, since Sarah was always home when I was, and it was clear she wanted my attention.

The argument began the evening I came home to find the television sitting on the piano, an open coke can next to it. I had never lost my temper with Sarah, but that night something exploded in me. I picked up the TV and almost threw it to the floor, took the coke and poured it down the sink, found a chamois and some lemon oil and began to carefully rub away the silver ring of water stain and the tiny scratches left by the TV. I was so angry it was difficult to look at her. For the first time, I raised my voice to her, demanding to know what she was thinking.

When she started to cry, it hurt my heart. I put down the chamois, gathered her in my arms and told her I was sorry.

She told me, between sobs, that she was sick of competing with a piano, that it was a big ugly freak that took up all the space and air and life in the living room. She told me it collected dust. She told me she was trying to make this our flat, but the piano insisted that it was only mine.

I held her and stroked her and murmured into her hair.

"I want you to get rid of the piano," she whispered.

I guided her to the bedroom. We made love *lento* this time, *doloroso*. When she fell asleep, I sat at the Bösendorfer, my fingers moving softly on her keys, pantomiming Mozart's Concert #20 in D Minor, too sad to even cry.

I left early the next morning, before she awoke. I returned that night, anxious to put all this behind us, carrying roses and chocolates. She was happy for the presents, but she told me she meant it. I needed to dispose of the Bösendorfer this week, or she would leave me the next day. She would not be swayed.

I told her we could rearrange the flat to her liking. She said it would never work. I proposed we move. She said I was missing the point. I told her the Bösendorfer reminded me of Uncle Samuel. She said he was dead and she was very much alive. I said I didn't know how to get rid of a Bösendorfer. She suggested Craig's List.

While Sarah sleeps, I tiptoe to the living room, put my fingers gently on those old ivory keys, lay my cheek on her soft sweet finish.

The Trajectory of Her Legs

Kristin Berger

The pedals have been slipping
under her booted will to turn corners,
stretch into longer and longer afternoons.
Not one notch, or two, but three
full clinks the toptube lengthens.
The bike adjusted, for now,
to this lanky new girl-body.

Fingers are counted upon, words
slip from her lips like pigeons arcing,
white-bellied notes above the wire.
I do nothing but hold
back. These growing pains
are like the stretch-marks I didn't know
I would one day welcome,
a map to trace the moments between
coming, going,
and soon-to-be gone.

Peanut Butter Neglect

Miriam Feder

For a lonely, only child, an invitation to someone's house for lunch was both a social opportunity and an anthropological experience. In my study, I was amazed to find that many mothers served what I thought of as the white lunch: a tall glass of milk with a sandwich on white bread. It was a mixed blessing. I hated the milk, but the sandwich was an exotic delight. Between perfect identical white spongy layers, I'd find a thin strip of something pink. It didn't look anything like a sandwich at my house.

When we became big kids in middle school, we ate in a cafeteria. Even lunch could be a source of embarrassment. I was suddenly measured against what "everybody else" had in her lunchbox. Yet again, I did not measure up.

Everybody else's lunch had a perfect white square that floated out of a small individual sandwich bag. The popular girls in my class had waxed paper bags.

The white square would be cut in half, to reveal two perfect bands, one violet and one creamy brown. I admired how evenly the grape jelly would saturate the white sponge, moistening it just enough to make it edible. The creamy peanut butter was applied with expert strokes stretching it to each corner, just like on TV. Most admirably, this sandwich remained stable when bitten.

How could I get my mother to reproduce this? My mother grew up across the Atlantic in a land bereft of peanut butter, white bread and grape jelly. For her, assimilation had already turned out to be a cruel trick. What could she possibly know about fitting in?

I'd inhale deeply before venturing into my disheveled paper bag. First, the sandwich bag was all wrong. It could be any plastic bag that found its way into the house, usually cradling my Dad's stiff shirt or the Tribune. These bags were huge, unwieldy and, by the time they reached the cafeteria, sticky inside and out. The sandwich didn't float out—often the bag would have to be removed from the sandwich. After this surgery, my hands, sometimes up to the forearms, would be sticky and dangerous, attracting napkins and transferring permanent purple ooze. (Finally my mother did discover Baggies—a great relief for both of us. I could sacrifice the finer point of waxed paper.)

But then the really embarrassing part emerged—the sandwich. This was made of two irregular slices of hard, seed-laden, black bread. They received uneven applications of chunky peanut butter and slid against each other like restless tectonic plates.

Moments into the bite, the bread released its magma: a writhing core of European fruit preserves. Black currant seeds would spill over the rubbery crusts onto the tray. The odd strawberry or rind oozed and slithered across brown mountains and valleys, sometimes shooting right out onto the table.

This sandwich was my immigrant mother's struggle. I pleaded for peanut butter sandwiches but she feared serving peanut butter to her only child was a sign of laziness, or worse, cheapness. However, fruit preserves! Now here was something a European could take pride in, embellish, indulge. She could atone for her peanut butter neglect.

I ate it. Of course I ate it; it was delicious. The nutty mixture of grains and seeds augmented the peanut butter, worthy ally to the large, carefully selected fruits.

I ate it and struggled to control it. I stole glances at the popular kids eating their cool, calm amethyst beauties.

I'd give Mom more instruction tonight. Tomorrow I might have one less thing to be self-conscious about.

Hot Day in the Garment District

Lee Haas Norris

1955, the summer between my sophomore and junior years at Barnard: a hot, sticky New York July and August spent shuttling among airless showrooms in the garment district of the West 30s. I'd been hired by the Ford agency as a dress model to show out-of-town buyers how the fall junior line from Suzy Perette and her peers would look on normal-sized girls. Native New Yorker though I was, I'd known the garment industry at a remove, mostly from those of my classmates whose fathers were in it. That summer the clogged side streets, the incessant shouting matches between drivers of double-parked apparel trucks, the dresses and coats swaying from handcarts defiantly crossing honking cars, the office workers clumped and schmoozing on sidewalks became my daily world.

On days when no buyers showed up I'd be assigned sixth-grade filing tasks. It was impossible not to eavesdrop on the coffee-break talk coming from back rooms with opened doors. Face averted, my eyes widened as I heard about one design firm's double set of books; another's special gifts to certain auditors; and how a well-known designer stood transfixed in horror when her business-partner husband told her in front of the employees that he'd be accompanying her on her vacation to Mexico. Rumor had it she'd been planning to make the trip with her boyfriend. The sheltered daughter of modest civil servants, I thrilled at this font of delicious gossip.

In late August I was assigned to a firm for three days—Rothman Brothers Furs on West 35th Street. It was a small operation: a cache of minks and ermines in two unremarkable rooms a few doors down from the Empire State Building. One brother, tall and mournful, was the financial brains of the pair. The other, Marvin, was squat, simian-faced, and only a few inches taller than I was. Black wiry hair sprouted from his open shirt, thick arms from his rolled-up sleeves, and successful persuasion from his voice. Sales was in his blood. Seven buyers came in three days and none left without an order.

I spent my spare time amusing myself with copies of *Women's Wear Daily* and the *Racing Form*. Towards the end of the third day, after a buyer from Cedar Rapids had left, I stood alone in the empty showroom, the luxurious mink over my underwear, the way furs got modeled then, with nothing to detract from the line of the garment—just the bra, underpants, garter belt, nylons, and pointed-toed heels.

"Don't take it off yet." I heard Marvin's thick voice just behind me. I turned toward him. He held me by the mink's collar. "Please." Oddly, the word actually *was* please. "Open it and let me see your breasts." Let him see my breasts! This man I'd met three days ago, a man old enough to be my father. Desire was in his eyes and voice. I was, at least technically, still a virgin. I needn't dwell on how incredulous this will sound today to any woman under 50, but I did as he asked. Marvin drew my breasts outside the black lace cups, put his lips to my nipples. Breathing hard he kissed them one by one, then went no further. Instead, with a quiet touch of his salesman's pitch, he offered to set me up in an apartment in Queens as his part-time girlfriend; he was of course married with children. He'd pay half of my college tuition. I'd be under no obligation. "No, no," I stammered in shock, I couldn't, I wouldn't. He sighed, but wasn't surprised. "No, of course you couldn't and of course you wouldn't. But here's my card, if you ever change your mind."

Hanging onto the strap of the uptown Broadway local on my way home I could think of nothing else, all that night and for days afterward. It was the first time I'd been wanted so nakedly by anyone, least of all an older man, and now, blushing with incomprehension, I found myself wanting him back and knowing I would never act on that desire. I kept my would-be lover's card, but even though people in the garment business crossed paths daily in 7th Avenue coffee shops, I never saw Marvin again. Two weeks later, however, I didn't hesitate to shed the final technicality with my delighted boyfriend.

Getting There

imagine how it will go from now on

Getting There

Jo Barney

Even as he gets himself hunched under the car, his knee aching and sticking straight out in plain sight, his hip lodged against the rear tire in the way he has imagined it, Frank knows it won't work. Edie might be batty, but she can still see.

As he expects, his wife comes thrashing around the back of the car, telling him to get up. "What are you doing?" she scolds, sounding like a mother again. "You're driving me crazy."

He considers the truth in that statement as he scoots his butt forward, dragging a leg along the driveway, and gets up on all threes, the bad knee not worth a damn. "I was checking the muffler."

"I could have run over you!"

He flinches as her bony knuckles whap the dust off his pants. That, of course, had been the idea, to get run over. Hearing his wife's ragged gasps as they walk up the path to the house, he knows he ought tell her he's sorry, that he didn't mean to frighten her, but then she'd ask why he did it in the first place. At the moment, the ache in his knee makes him think mostly about where he is putting his foot, and he can hardly understand it himself.

"It's okay, Edie," he says.

The sunlight hurts his eyes and he squints against it as they go into the house. In the kitchen, the usual foggy cloud in the center of his sight offers glimpses of the stove and fridge. He moves into the living room, finds his easy chair, drops into its familiar hug, and presses the lever that raises his legs up to where the knee no longer has any work to do. A stab of his finger brings on a slow parade of words from his latest tape, and he closes his aching eyes against the fluttering gray void and his ears to his wife's voice meandering in the kitchen.

Edie has always talked a lot. From day one, the minute he walked in the door after work, covered with gray overspray from the ships he was hired to paint and only wishing for a hot bath and the one drink he allowed himself, she'd start in, leaving him gasping, drowning in the trivia of her day. Somewhere along the line he learned that if he didn't meet her eyes, he wouldn't have to answer her. When their daughter Sarah was young, Edie had someone to talk to and the house took on a rhythm that did not include him. His fault, he guessed. "Your father's very quiet, that's all" he once overheard his wife tell Sarah as the two of them did the dishes. "Doesn't mean he doesn't love you."

These days, when Sarah stops by after work on Fridays, he can't hear a word she says as she kisses him hello, his blotchy vision obscuring all but a piece of hand or foot, his hearing aid useless in the muffled undertow of her words. Her voice was always soft, like a breeze, compared to Edie's hurricane. When the two women sit over coffee in the kitchen, their voices churning up the air between them, he's sure they still talk about him.

"Frank. I need for you to listen." Edie is shaking him, the tape turned off, a lamp lit over his chair. Her hand tightens his arm, her agitation quivering between her knee and his.

"I got lost."

"Yeh?"

"I had my appointment, you know, for Dr. Wilton. Because of that bump on my place down there. I told you about it. I got there okay, and then, when I tried to leave the parking lot, I couldn't think of which way. I went right and didn't recognize anything, so I turned around and went the other direction. Nothing. No Levenson's Cleaners, where I always turn. No A&W. I turned around again and couldn't even find the clinic, just tall buildings."

"So you asked?" Frank knows she didn't.

"I pulled over and started crying."

"Yeh?"

"Then I stopped crying and told myself to get a grip."

He can imagine it.

"I saw the bakery. I saw the Doug firs behind it. I knew our house was under the trees. I just had to get to the trees. Then," Edie sighs, "I found us!" Her hand leaves his arm, rests on her flat warm breast as she catches her breath.

Frank picks up his pipe, searches his shirt pocket for his lighter. "I keep telling you to write down street names." He considers adding that she should face it, she shouldn't drive anymore, but she has gotten up, is leaving the room. His pipe whistles as he sucks on it.

"Don't you want to know what the doctor said?" She is standing beside him again.

"Sure." He takes a last pull on the pipe and brushes a hand against the singe he smells smoldering in his shirt front. He hopes that Edie won't notice.

"He said that I am dried up, and the bump is like a…" she hesitates, "a callus, needs to be softened up."

"Callus."

"Nice young doctor, but a little rough, he said I should use a cream…." She holds up the box, aims it towards the edge of his eye so that he can see it. "Hormone something. I told him I was not into hormones. Look at my file, I said, breast cancer at 76, after a dose of hormones. Give me a break, I am still feeling my boobs every day, but he said this was not the same, only makes the callus soft." She waits for him to say something.

"Sounds okay," he decides. What does he know?

"I'm glad about the cream," she answers. "Maybe it will help." Her voice is her young Edie voice, innocent, sexy, offering the world to him sixty years ago, offering only herself now. He almost sees the curve of her lips, her cheeks breaking into the soft ravines of a smile.

The horniness started last summer. She had slipped her hand between his legs in the middle of the night, whispering please, willing him to wake up. His penis, long unused to fingers other than his own, rose up, quivered and leaked, retreated and lay silent like the rest of him. Gently, she placed his hand on her body, and he searched with his fingertips for the wetness until she sighed and turned away. Lately, lying next to this new, restless Edie, he thinks what a cruel twist it is that a sad forgetfulness has brought her back to him like this.

Frank shifts his weight, tries to think about something else. "So you're okay?"

"I just told you, didn't you listen?" Then she veers off in a new direction. "Time for dinner?" she asks.

"Or...?"

"Or lunch?"

"Look at the clock, Edie," he prompts, pointing at the mantle.

"Dinner, right?" She sounds pleased with herself.

"Right, dinner." No telling what she'll come up with to eat. She can't follow recipes anymore and every meal is a surprise. He sits back and presses the tape's green button.

"Chicken noodle," she says a few minutes later. "From a can." She arranges the tray at his side.

"I can still taste." He takes a bite of his sandwich, chewing it on the right side where he has the most teeth. If she's watching, she'll start in about dentures, he thinks, but instead she murmurs, "It's really weird. Maybe I *am* crazy."

"What?"

"I can't remember if I've had lunch, but just out of nowhere, I remember things, from a long time ago, like little movies except I feel them, like it's happening right now."

"Like what?"

"Like the time you cried."

He knows what's coming and tries to head her off. "When I saw Sarah the first time? You laughed at me."

"No, I mean later. You know. I just couldn't understand why you would do that, tell me you were going fishing and then be with that woman, that Janice."

"That was a long time ago, Edie." He, not Edie, has forgotten the woman's name.

"And when I asked you what was going on, you lied, said nothing was going on, but I knew, remember? I thought I would die."

"Edie...."

"I cried for a week, wondering what I had done wrong. And then one night, when you reached for me, I smelled her on you again. Remember?"

He does remember. "That was a bad time, Edie." He feels her get up out of her chair, kneel beside him, touch his temple, trace a finger like a tear down his cheek.

"We've had a good life, though, I think. Don't you?" Her hand travels across his chest, towards his belt.

He takes her fingers in his, presses them to his lips, catches the faint scent of the lotion she uses each morning. "A pretty good life," Frank says, surprised at the small jolt of pleasure these words give him. Forty years ago he couldn't have imagined it.

That night Edie had risen up from her pillow, her breasts sliding against the silk of her nightgown as she turned to him, her voice, low and foreign. "Why?"

He thought of the way his body nearly exploded every time he knocked on that apartment door and heard that happy, "Frankie!" felt the warm arms around his neck. Like a young man. Like there was more to be had. Like he was still himself. But, at that moment, looking at Edie, at the pain reddening her eyelids, her trembling lips, he knew he would never be able to explain. When he wept, Edie believed it was because he was sorry he had hurt her and she held his cheek in her hand.

Edie's fingers slip away as she stands up. "Garbage day?"

"No, today's Tuesday, Edie."

They used to joke about it, the way people joke about dying or going bald or wearing diapers. "I've lost my keys again. Must be Old Timers," she'd say. He and Edie stopped laughing the day the empty pot on the burner burst into flames and turned the kitchen ceiling black with soot.

"I'm losing it," she said, and their doctor agreed.

Scribbling into his prescription pad, he added, "Might be years of good living yet," but Frank did not believe it, not the good living part.

Edie had always skittered about her days creating "what if's" and endless lists. "Take it easy," he'd tell her. "Life's too short." Her almost burning down the house changed that. From then on, he took over as worrier, his mind turning over the facts like puzzle pieces, looking for the one that would fit, bring some sense back to their life. This much he knew: his retirement check barely covered their bills and definitely would not cover the $5,000 a month Old Timers were charged. The missing piece, he realized, was the fact that he did not want to stick around any longer, not blind and deaf and no good to anyone. But their insurance policy was very clear. Demises paid $200,000. Suicide paid one-half. It couldn't look like he'd done himself in.

The car thing was a bad idea, at least with Edie behind the wheel. He leans back into his lounger, closes his eyes, and puts his feet up as his wife clears away their dishes.

"I'm so glad you've decided to go out for walks," Edie says, her thin arm resting on his as they move along the sidewalk. He props his elbow against his hip, not sure who is supporting whom.

"Just remember to pick up your feet a little more so that you don't stumble. I wish you could see the Jensen's hydrangeas," she rambles on in her careless way. "They're bright maroon. Wonder what they put in the soil to get that color. Didn't you use to put nails under ours? What would make maroon?"

At the edges of the gray blot, he can see green grass, and tree trunks, and parked cars, or elephants, whatever. He spots the maroon.

"I don't know," he answers, thinking of their dog Buster, buried under the giant zinnias in the back yard. "Maybe old dog bones."

"We're at Second Street, already. Should we turn back?"

Her knowing the name of the street pleases him, makes him hesitate, and finally he is able to say, "Let's go across to the park." They have walked every day this week, and now, on Friday, the day he has chosen, his knee is killing him. Not enough, of course. That's the trouble. He wobbles a little over an uneven spot and Edie stiffens her hold on him.

"Are you sure?"

"Yep." He straightens his shoulders and raises his arm a fraction of an inch. He is as sure as he'll ever be.

"Next time we'll use your cane," she says. They stop at the curb.

The cars coming from the left do not enter his fringe of vision until they are almost in front of him and then they disappear. He takes his hand from Edie's arm and puts it into his pocket so that she won't feel it trembling. When a green blur flashes at the edge of gray, he draws a quick breath. This is it, he tells himself, and he bends his good knee and plunges into the street. A swipe of metal throws him to the asphalt, a wail of brakes leaves him to understand that he is not dead yet.

Edie, clutching at his collar, keens softly into his ear.

"My God! Dad walked right into my car." Incredibly, Sarah's voice, an anxious hearable screech, sweeps through him, a hand, hers, touches his forehead, dabs something at it. "What in hell was he thinking about?"

Frank pulls himself up onto an elbow, probes at his bloody eyebrow with his fingertips. "I'm okay," he says, like always unable to explain himself. "Let's go home." He rolls onto his hip, gets his knee bent right and tries to rise up.

"Frank, don't. You might have hurt yourself." Edie still clings to him, pressing him down. Then her words are directed upward towards the shadow hovering above them. "This wasn't your fault, dear. My husband stepped right into your way. He doesn't see well, you know."

After a moment, Sarah responds in a calm undecipherable murmur, and he is lifted to his feet and led to the car. Doors slam, the motor rumbles, the car begins to move. Behind him, Edie leans forward, grasps the back of his seat, her words drifting in an anxious whirl past him, towards Sarah. "I feel as if I know you. Do you live near here?"

Frank closes his eyes, tries to imagine how it will go from now on. His daughter's hand brushes his thigh, remains there. He marvels at the comfort of her touch and his fingers seek hers, entwine themselves with hers, and he gives himself over to her.

Rivers

Kristina Bak

I'd become a woman of temperate habits and cautious gestures. I almost believed I wasn't afraid, only following acquired wisdom, the day I set out in search of rafting skills. Motherhood had taught me to look both ways and be prepared, and that there was a class for everything from childbirth to dying. Posters at the outdoor sports store in the mall reminded me that adventure had become a commodity, and I was about to buy. In illustration of my nonchalance I browsed racks of clothing lining faux stone walls. Black synthetics looked more suited to a Navy Seals mission than a guided river trip. Video screens played a mesmerizing sequence of whitewater scenes, none of which I could imagine surviving.

"Help you ma'am?" A Tennessee drawl far from home.

Perhaps lunch first, time to think about this. Four men lounged behind the counter, Tennessee the eldest of them, still a couple of decades younger than I. They stared at me, all casual slow smiles—the shape of a woman's dream.

"What d'you need?" Tennessee ready to accommodate.

"Lessons, for a trip in July. Just whitewater basics, survival, that sort of thing."

All four men nodded. I felt a juvenile relief; I'd passed the first test.

"Great! We teach our kayak rolls in the public pool this time of year. Indoors. Sunday evenings at six."

I thought rafts, not kayaks, but the men were grinning now in a friendly way. And why not? Kayaks or rafts, they all go on the water. I left the store with a business card in hand. On the back scrawled in faint ballpoint: Sunday, 6pm, Brett.

Sunday was winter's worst day with wind-driven bullets of sleet, full dark by four-thirty, streets floes of slush by six. The distance between my car and the locker room felt geographic: I walked through longitudes and latitudes to the warmth of tropic seas, and finally stood in my yellow swimsuit, toes curled over the pool's concrete edge. Like mer-people, only half human-half boat, kayakers rolled and spun, splashed and rowed (I would learn to say paddled). Their faces shone with a self-absorbed bliss I'd seen mostly in children.

I found Brett, or Brett found me; how it happened was lost in the unexpected urgency of my desire to slither into the spray skirt, wedge my knees, brace my feet, stretch the skirt over the opening of the kayak, grasp the paddle with its long tips up, and at last launch myself into the pool. All sound and movement around me stopped, even time. Someone I didn't know breathed for me, a long sigh, drawn from some part of my body I didn't own. I'd at once come home and dropped free fall into a foreign sphere.

"Ready to learn the wet exit?"

Like a carnival ride beginning, kayaks moved around me again in joyful anarchy, picking up speed and volume. Brett stood close, chest deep in the water.

"Exit. From the kayak? I've only just gotten in."

"It's the first safety thing you have to learn, so you don't get trapped if you flip."

Brett had good cheekbones, sharp and angled in an otherwise gentle face. That was what I noticed then. I practiced tipping my kayak until I hung head down beneath the water, at first in awful panic, then counting to five, then ten, popping loose the spray skirt, slipping free and rising to the surface, boat in tow, climbing back in to repeat the sequence. Brett ran a litany of encouraging words.

"Fine. You're doing good. It's all body memory. Kayakers are simple people. We get the memory in our body so we don't have to think about it anymore. Here, take my hands."

Brett held out his open hands to me, palms up on top of the water. An Asian man, long black hair flying, cartwheeled his kayak at the other end of the pool. Waves rocked my boat. I turned to the side and laid my hands in Brett's. Body memory. How long had it been since I touched a half-naked young man? The thought startled me. It wasn't a thought I would recognize as mine, but Brett was right. The body has a memory of its own. At middle age I was tending to forget names of people in my outer circle of friendship, but I couldn't forget the carnality of youth.

"I'm sorry, what do I do?"

"This is the hip snap. Tip over until your face is on your hands, then roll back up with as little pressure as possible on my hands. Do it with your hips."

Hips, hands, my face in the water so near his belly. My confusion must have shown.

"It's all right, I won't let you go."

My body tipped, touched, snapped and struggled to roll its kayak shell while my mind worried its burden of doubt about trust and physicality, a caged animal so accustomed to imprisonment it can't recognize an open door.

Behind everything I did that week, my lesson ran in a constant loop. At my desk my hips twitched with a vestigial snap. I released the thread of conversations tipping my consciousness upside down in an imagined pool.

I drove to my second Sunday lesson through winter rain. It fell straight down, cold but not frozen, and ran through gutters in oil-slicked black streams. The water in the pool seemed a different element, warm blue, bright with lights that sparkled in almost convincing imitation of the sun.

"This one will fit you better."

Brett groped inside the new red kayak, past my pale thighs, to tuck foam blocks beneath my feet. I flinched from his touch, but he was as dispassionate as a gynecologist, and right about the boat; with the blocks in place it felt like an extension of my body. Brett's arms came around me from behind to help stretch the tight new spray skirt. I reminded myself this was not an embrace. And then we were in the water and it was all happening again, an infusion of delight so divergent from my ordinary days that I may as well have been on a different planet.

Everything was in motion. Sitting still I rocked and drifted. Paddling a zigzag course across the pool I flew, seeing around me a mirror lake, shores overhung with dark spruce, until I bumped and scraped along the pool side. Brett adjusted my grip on the paddle. His hand brushed the length of my arm. I told myself it was a random gesture, but the body knows no logic.

"We'll have you in the river by spring."

I pictured him frolicking like an otter.

"Is that how your life is? Do you play in the water all the time?"

His smile lifted the corners of his eyes.

"I try to arrange it that way."

The last weeks of winter brought no respite from the rain, only length-ening hours of gray between reluctant dawn and nightfall. My Sunday eve-nings were a beacon promising color and light at the end of a muddy slog. Brett guided me through my lessons in incremental steps, each achievement trumped by a new demand. Our conversation became more intimate, shared reminiscences of our first sessions as something belonging to just the two of us, our general states of mind and well-being. Innocuous conversation, free of innuendo, seductive in its innocence lapped by the warm water of the pool. The distance for me between sensual and erotic was never great; I found my excitement in the new ways I was learning to move my body with the kayak slipping into another bodily curiosity.

Brett was a tall man, robust and deep-chested, with a manner at once deferential and protective. I let myself forget, for the time we were together in the pool, that I was paying for his attention and undeniable (though I cringed from the thought) boyish charm. I plotted to ferret out his age. Sure-ly older than my eldest.

"How long have you been kayaking? How old were you when you first learned?"

I did the math. Twenty-two years younger than I. My curiosity didn't abate, but I cultivated a jocular manner, a harder voice. I scanned my body language to edit out the vocabulary of futile invitation. It seemed to me there was no one else over thirty in the pool, certainly no one my age. Brett stared at me uncomprehending when the subject came up, as it did only when I raised it myself.

"What difference does it make? People ask me how old I am sometimes. I tell them whatever age my environment lets me be."

I admired his attitude. I would have held it myself a few years back, but that had changed as I approached fifty and caught mortality signaling from my mirror. I'd stumbled into a duplicity of perception. In my dreams I lived in my lissome youth, but that wasn't the face or form I carried into the wak-ing world.

Brett introduced another new step on our fifth Sunday. I was to tip my kayak until I rolled against him where he stood up to his neck in the pool to steady me, then right myself with no help from my hands. I was sure I could do it; I was eager to try. I tipped, my shoulder grazed Brett's chest, but the thrust of my hips only turned me upside down. Brett's arms closed around me under the water; he fumbled for a hold. His hands slipped up my torso to cup the lower part of my breasts. I felt him hesitate, then slide his hands away to the hull of my kayak to help me roll up out of his arms.

"Again. Do it again."

Four, five, six times we repeated the exercise, Brett's caresses and my response to them unacknowledged, as though nothing that happened under water counted above. Each time my performance deteriorated until it became obvious that another repetition wouldn't improve my skills. My bodily memory was on overload, my dream-self ascendant. I gasped and coughed, pretending it was only because I'd breathed water.

"I think I'd better practice paddling for awhile."

I met Brett later outside the locker room. We stood facing each other, smelling of chlorine, he like a large little boy with his shirt buttoned up to his neck. I offered him his money. He shook his head.

"No charge for this evening. I don't think we accomplished very much."

"No, I guess we didn't."

That night I dreamed of rivers, water flowing over earth and stone—deep smooth jade green, glacial blue beneath lips of ice, white and loud with danger, shallows clear as air. I dreamed of rivers caught between walls of sun, rivers devouring tributaries and running wide into the sea, winding sluggish through a tunnel of trees and diving headlong off escarpments into roaring pools. I dreamed voices of rivers invisible in the night, and woke with a hunger for rivers as sudden and inexplicable as sexual desire.

A day of false spring tantalized with sun that set the streets steaming and still lingered behind the Olympic Range when I drove to the pool for lesson number six. I avoided Brett's eyes, and perhaps he avoided mine. We were

71

brisk in our speech and attentive to the business of boating. I heard a note of distance in Brett's voice.

"Remember the kayak roll is eighty percent mental and twenty percent physical. You have to believe that you'll do it, let go of old ideas, don't hurry. Take your time under the water until the hip snap is a conscious decision, then begin the snap and turn your head and your eyes. Nothing will happen if you don't move your eyes."

We were both encased in our kayaks tonight, no risk of our bodies touching. I rested one hand on the bow of his boat and tipped myself upside down into the silence of the water. I felt my body float into its new position, the stillness that leads to motion, then thrust my knee up to begin the snap and turned my head to look over my shoulder. The simple gesture, my looking in a new direction, moved my whole body. I rolled up on my own as though I'd always known how. Brett laughed at my look of surprise, and I laughed with him. I pushed my wet hair out of my face and readjusted my noseplugs. The rivers rushed out before me, all the rivers I had yet to know, new routes opening within me where I'd thought all of my territories had been mapped and explored. I felt poised on the brink of rapids. Brett pushed our kayaks apart.

"Again. Do it again."

Gratitude for the Mending

Lilian Sarlos

Another Fall of our love passing
Winter falling soft, dark
Spring rutting gone
Summer ease a warm memory

Fall harvest reaped—
seeds and leaves
drop, pummeled by rain
and dark

Rest now
ripeness inside the walls
slow gratitude for the arrival of winter

this winter of having
a thing or two to share.

Slow down
feel the blue gray clouds
rest from the rush of fullness
always center,
every day a glowing, searing first—

first journey,
first love, first sex, first marriage,
first house, first dog, first tree,
first boy, first girl.

One year
not knowing what next
we broke.

This winter we bathe in gratitude
for the mending
in gratitude for knowing a thing or two
if not what is next.

The Highway

Rhea Wolf

It seems like Exodus
but mad, fleeing
from our own tyranny
the cities we've built
to more cities.
These screeching hungry lines
caravans lit up for miles
in such straight lines
in heartless shuddering.
The earth is concrete
and not moving underneath
anymore moving only
on the surface
as rubber paw meets
the new path

and it is endless.

I sit overlooking Interstate 10
between Phoenix and Tucson
nothing between but the road
its steely fauna
and lonely Picacho Peak
looking out
unnoticed
when all eyes obey
the straight line
and the car moving
just ahead
taillights flashing
swerving dance
hypnotic passing
billboardspeak trance.

Refugee movements
(away and to)
we've made of our lives.

Blind exodus now
we fear tyrants
not the gods
but terror and poverty and nature
the appearance of lack
the appearance
when our covers
are torn back
and even our lovers
never see this
in seats beside us
passengers of our escaping
holding our hands
eyes on the road
singing along to the radio
racing along
four lane interstate
inner-state quaking
helpless exodus
that isn't
holy anymore.

It's just something we do
movement is what we do
movement is what we are.

Welfare-kid Lies

Caren Coté

As soon as Pamela heard I wasn't going to see my mom on Mother's Day she suggested we go to brunch together, a "Not Yet Mothers" brunch, she said. She chose a trendy little restaurant in the hippest part of Berkeley. We sat outside, at a beautiful round table covered with an Irish lace table-cloth, a small vase of lilacs in the center. Big white picture-clouds floated in the blue sky. Halfway through our Caesar salads I asked what her mom was doing today and she blew my mind.

"My mom killed herself," she said.

"I thought you had a perfect childhood!"

"I did. This was in college. Our family life was always great."

I froze, my fork halfway to my mouth, and sat quietly, digesting the revelation. Pamela had been my middle-class role model since I lucked out and got my job as a clerk, two cubicles down from her at a busy accounting office. She grew up in Mill Valley, went to UC Berkeley, and slid into an entry-level job the week after graduation. Me, I'm from South Hayward, and not the one good neighborhood. I earned an Associates degree in bookkeeping at Chabot Community College in four years while working fifty hours a week at two jobs, a liquor store and a flower shop. With a degree in my hand I thought my hardest work was over, but I was only partly right.

Pam grabbed my wrist and shook it, I yelped and my fork went flying onto the table next to ours. She threw her head back and laughed and it was so un-self-conscious that the four generations of moms and daughters at that table joined her. I would've been happy to disappear.

"Earth to Carrie, come in Carrie!" Pam laughed. "Where'd you go?"

"Oh, nowhere. I was just thinking it's strange that I've known you for almost three years and I don't really know much about you."

She waved that away with a manicured hand, flipped her brown shoulder length hair back and popped a crouton into her mouth.

"You know it all. Basically." She ate the last bite of her Caesar salad and scanned the room like a hungry cat. "I wonder where that waiter with the cute tushie is, dessert sounds good."

I did some quick math in my head to see if I could afford dessert too.

A few minutes later the waiter sat one of those big, sloppy-looking chocolate cake-and-ice cream desserts in front of us with two forks.

"Who are you to talk anyway?" Pamela asked. "I've never even seen your apartment."

She did that, continued conversations that we'd left off minutes, or even hours, before, just like someone on a TV show. Maybe she'd watched too much TV growing up. Most of the time my family didn't have a TV. I told everyone at school it was because my parents didn't believe in TV, in a hippie kind of way, but nobody bought it; they all recognized the welfare-kid lies because they told them too.

"My place? It's nothing special, you're not missing anything." I searched for a new topic.

"It's not a big deal if it's small, my place is small too, but cozy." Pam's idea of small was her three-bedroom house in a decent neighborhood in San Francisco. If she ever saw my one-bedroom, five hundred square-foot apartment on the third floor of an old concrete box of a building a few miles south of where the Berkeley border ends, it would be against my will.

"Why did your mom kill herself?" I wanted to clap my hand over my mouth. I hadn't meant to say that out loud. "If you don't mind my asking."

"It's okay. My dad's mother moved in with us—my mom had to care for her as if she were an infant because Grandma had Alzheimer's—and after a while mom just couldn't take it anymore. She went down to the basement and hung herself."

Pam spooned dessert into her mouth and swallowed it sensually, moaning, as if we'd just been talking about men. She did it again.

"Your parents' house has a basement?"

"Mom insisted Daddy have one excavated. She was raised in the Midwest and said homes without basements weren't civilized."

"Oh." I wasn't sure it would stay down, but I tried to keep my mouth full of cake and ice cream anyway so I wouldn't ask any more inappropriate questions. The dessert was only so big.

"So, where did you say your mom went this year?" I let her change the subject—gladly.

"Up north, to visit my brother."

"Cool, where does he live, Sunol?"

"No, farther north." I'd ask another suicide question before I'd tell her the truth: that my brother was in San Quentin serving fifteen to twenty-five years for a half-dozen drug- and violence-related crimes.

"Oooh, Seattle? That's a great city—as long as you're there one of the two sunny days they get a year!" She laughed and I encouraged her by laughing along. What did I know? I'd never been farther from South Hayward than Sacramento, the '76 truck stop on Interstate 80 to be exact.

"He lives in Sacramento, but we don't see him very much." Anyone with my last name would have to sneak up on me.

We finished dessert. Pam invited me along on her clothes-shopping trip, but I begged off blaming my student loan payment. My way was back on the bus (two buses) south on San Pablo Avenue to my neighborhood, and off the bus in front of the liquor store. In the time it took me to buy a pint of cheap whiskey and a one-liter bottle of generic cola I was propositioned twice in Spanish and threatened once in English.

I walked the three blocks to my building and wondered if I should stop hanging out with Pam. Friday afternoon, when I got home from work, I was content with my apartment, my furniture, my life that I'd made and paid for on my own. But right then all I could think of was a cozy three bedroom house in San Francisco. I sat on my faded green couch drinking straight out of both bottles and furnished and decorated that house. Modern Gypsy Biker style—faded green couches and yellow vinyl kitchen chairs decorated with electrical tape were not included, soft black leather furniture that hugged you when you sat on it, lots of dark purple and gold velvet and fringe, and glass tables held up by sculptures of bald eagles. Very plush. While I was at it, I decided to make up people to share the house with me: a husband with a good job who never hit, a couple of kids who played soccer and went to ballet class, and a brother and parents who came over every week for Sunday dinner and made appropriate conversation.

Halfway through the bottle, a mom appeared hanging from a beam in the living room ceiling of that dream house and I couldn't get her out. If someone put a gun to my head and made me tell them if Pam's mom's suicide made me sad or happy, I'd probably be shot. I've never known much about being normal, but I knew enough to be sure my feelings about Pam having such a big skeleton in her closet were not normal.

A knock on the dingy wall next to where my head rested startled me out of my daydreaming. It was Nikki signaling that her husband was off to work and I should come over to hang out. She let out a whoop when I pushed her door open, just like she was at a concert or something. Her TV had Cops playing too loud, and when I plopped down on her 1970s-reject orange striped couch a puff of dust poofed up beside me. My second home.

"So, chica, you have fun at your brunch?"

I laughed and rolled my eyes, she cursed under her breath in Spanish and laughed along with me. Nikki's mom crossed the border from Mexico one night while she was very pregnant. The blond-haired and blue-eyed nurse at the hospital was named Nikki. Mrs. Chavez thought that was a good American name and gave it to her daughter.

"Why do you hang out with that stuck-up gabacha? If she knew you were only passing as white, she'd never even say 'Hi' or 'Fuck you' to you. You know I'm right."

"It's not passing when you're half of something. How do you think I got the name 'Miller' anyway?"

"Okay, okay, Corazon Miller, white as flour!" She exaggerated her accent when she said that, especially my first name which I did not use anymore. I got my first apartment two days after graduating high school, if you can call a closet with a toilet an apartment, and I left my old name with my family. I wanted something more normal than Corazon, so I chose Carrie, like the white girl in that movie who killed everyone in her high school class. "It's a tragedy how you turned your back on your heritage," Nikki said.

I laughed so loud and long that tears fell out of my eyes and Mrs. Rodriguez next door pounded on the wall to shut me up. My dad, according to my mom's sister, Tia Rose, beat my mom "to within an inch of her life" when she named my brother Miguel, and then again when she named me. He'd only married her because she forgot to take her pill sometimes and ended up with Miguel. When Miguel started running with the gang, Dad tried to beat some sense into him, but ended up with a knife in the gut and a son in prison covered with gang tattoos. Nikki knew all of my heritage, so I just passed her the bottles. She took a healthy swig of the whiskey and chased it with the weak cola.

"It's not like I have any trouble saying no, but every time Pam suggests something I just say okay without thinking."

"Trying to climb up that corporation ladder, huh?" She laughed.

"As if I could!"

"You don't think so, but I think so. You're the smartest person I know, you even went to college!"

"You could go back to school too, Nik, you're smart."

Something mean passed across her face.

"Not everybody is like you Carrie, with goals and shit. Quincy likes me here—not working, not in school—and that's fine by me." She smiled, took another swig of whiskey and chased it with cola, but her voice challenged me to disagree. I just took the bottle and drank so she could change the subject.

Frog Jump

Susan Prindle

Splat! She hit the wall with a thud. It was as if I went right along with her limp green body, shattering into pieces. We both slid to the ground, spreading lifeless in the hot sun.

They laughed. Everyone around me—my new husband, our friends, the others in the parking lot. They all joined in with beer-soaked laughter, while I stood there in shock. I didn't laugh.

I wanted to scream at them—Do you know what you just did? You goddamned pulled a frog from a pond, a cool stream where she was happy catching bugs and swimming in the cold water, you shoved her in your pocket, carried her around all day, sat on her, and now, you just threw her against a wall. She was almost gone anyway, hardly a breath left, dreams of water-splashed rocks and dragonflies and clear blue, almost gone.

I watched it all, she lying there in the graveled dirt, shriveling in the heat.

I tell you this—nothing has hurt me more than that moment, when I stood there and watched a beautiful green living thing thrown viciously against a concrete wall, guts splaying out, me keeping quiet, clenching my lips together to keep from screaming, and holding...holding...holding...like a pressure cooker. Keep the lid on. Don't let it explode like that frog, all those years ago, that I did not defend.

Getting Even

Mary Zelinka

"But he's not so big anymore," Beverly said. I pressed the phone to my ear. Her voice dropped every time she mentioned her father, as though afraid he could hear her. Raped by him over forty years before, Beverly still spent sleepless nights. I talked with her often during the years I worked overnights at the Center Against Rape and Domestic Violence.

"He's an old man now," she said. "He was so big when I was five, but I'm not five anymore. Maybe I should go see him to remind myself." She paused. "And I sure would like to get even somehow," she said.

"Hey, don't forget the best revenge is creating a good life." We laughed together.

The following week Beverly's words kept coming back to me. Maybe I needed to see my ex-husband again.

Twenty years had passed since we divorced, yet I still suffered nightmares. The dream was always the same: I'd be living my current life in Oregon, far from the days of Colorado and Jack. Then he'd walk into my house announcing, "It's time to go home now, Bear."

Jack always called me "Bear." I had been flattered when he first nicknamed me. But my renaming had been the beginning of my disappearance. By the time I left him, I didn't know what I felt, what I thought. I didn't even know what kind of music I liked anymore.

The scariest part of the nightmare was its realness. In the dream, I would look around my peaceful home; taking in the bulletin board covered with pictures of my friends, bookcases bursting with favorite titles, cassettes stacked next to my tape player. And then, with tears filling my eyes, I'd follow him out the door.

Five years after I had left him, he sent me a letter. His handwriting seemed to leap out of the mailbox. My body turned to lead. I dragged myself like a zombie back to the house. For two days that letter sat in my desk's bottom drawer before I opened it.

He was active in AA, he wrote. Three years clean and sober. Remarried his first wife. He'd love to hear from me.

Hot tears ran down my face as I ripped his words into tiny pieces and then rammed them down the garbage disposal. "Isn't that nice, that he's doing so well!" I screamed over the choking, grinding blades. My wooden spoon splintered as I jabbed at stray wet words. I left the disposal running long after the gears whirred empty.

Nowhere in that letter did he acknowledge hurting me.

Every time he had made fun of my stuttering in front of our friends I became more hesitant. Every time he shouted, "You are so goddamned stupid!" I questioned my sanity. Every time he raped me I wished I was dead.

By the time I left him my heart was paralyzed. Believing his judgment that I was an unfit mother, I let my first husband take custody of my nine-year-old son, Bob. I had nothing left to give anyone. I didn't even think I could take care of myself.

Instinctively, I knew I would be safer from Jack if there were a few states between us. So after selling most of my belongings, I turned my back on the aspen trees blazing gold in the mountains, and fled to Oregon.

A week after that late night hotline call from Beverly, I had another nightmare. But instead of the usual, it was a flashback. Rape. I awoke with a start, my pajamas drenched in cold sweat.

I needed to see Jack again. To see that he wasn't "so big." And yes, I wanted to get even.

I knew he still lived in Denver. I could stay with my best friend Sheila. After seeing Jack, Bob and I could backpack in Rocky Mountain National Park.

My stomach went cold just thinking about calling Jack to set up a meeting. I could barely hear the operator tell me his phone number, my heart thumped so loudly. I decided I'd better practice hearing his voice. It was only March; I had three months before my trip. I got a telephone recording device and one Saturday afternoon, with the sun shining safety over my backyard, I called. I clicked the recorder on as soon as the phone rang.

"Hello," the voice of my nightmares said. "You have reached the Bullard residence." Perfect! His answering machine! The pounding in my chest drowned out the rest of the message. At the sound of the beep I hung up.

I rewound the tape and listened to it. I played it every day until I could hear his voice with my normal heart rate.

Then I called, flipping on the recorder just in case I couldn't remember our conversation. Plus, I'd have proof if he yelled. Not like the old days when I wondered if I had only imagined his rages.

"Hello Jack, this is Mary." My pulse raced.

"Bear! Good to hear from you!"

"I go by Mary now," I said. I stood next to my dining room table, gripping the back of the chair.

"Of course. That would make sense." He sounded kind. Like he had when I first met him. "How are you? Still living in Oregon?"

"I am. And I'm doing well. But I'm putting my past to rest, and you're part of that."

He was silent.

"I'm planning a trip to Colorado in June. Will you be around so we can meet?"

"Well, sure." But he hesitated.

After we hung up, I sat down and rewound the tape. My voice was quiet, but I hadn't stuttered.

Over the next couple of months I replayed that tape often. And I practiced what I would say when we met. "Why didn't you ever apologize for all you did to me?" I'd shout. I imagined telling him how worthless he was—just as he had told me. I imagined him begging for my forgiveness.

I'd bring my tripod so I could take a picture of us together. I'd position him sitting. Then I'd set the timer and rush to stand behind him. Just when the tune announced the shutter about to flick, I'd strike a terrible pose over him. My face snarling, my hands raised over his head as though I were going to strike him. I'd have the picture blown up to an 8x10 so I could remember that now I was the strong one.

"I don't know why you need to see that guy," my son said one night on the phone as we planned our backpacking trip. "I was in Denver a couple of years ago and looked him up in the phone book. Then I thought, 'What do I have to say to him? Tell him he's a f-ing bastard?'"

"It's just something I have to do." I wound my finger through the loops in the phone cord.

"I'm afraid you'll get hurt," Bob said. "Let me go with you."

"I'll be OK. I need to do this on my own."

My friends worried too. "Will you be safe?" they asked.

But I wasn't afraid of Jack. I was afraid I'd turn back into that scared, stuttering, crazy-eyed woman I had been. That I'd become Bear again.

I drove the same route back to Colorado that I had driven twenty years before. Through the Columbia Gorge where the wind had blown so hard I had to fight to keep my van in the right lane. Through the Blue Mountains where I had gotten stuck in the snow. Idaho, where one gas station attendant forgot to put my gas cap back on. Utah, where frozen dead rabbits had littered the highway. Evanston, Wyoming where the sub-zero temperatures killed all but one of my house plants when I raced them into the motel.

When I turned at Cheyenne and headed south on 85 towards Denver, my heart swelled. The Platte River Valley spread out before me. Plowed fields glistened emerald in the sun and stretched towards the Rockies, deep purple under gathering dark clouds. Tears sprang to my eyes. "I want Colorado back!" I yelled, banging the heels of my hands on the steering wheel. "I have as much right to be here as he does!"

That night I called Jack from Sheila's.

"Well, gee, Mary," he said. "I'd love to see you, but we are going to Loveland tomorrow to spend the weekend at my mother's."

"No problem. I'm meeting Bob tomorrow afternoon in Estes Park. Loveland is right on the way."

He gave me directions, but I knew he didn't want to see me. That night anxious dreams kept me restless and awake.

His mother's neighborhood hadn't changed. Giant spruce and heavy old cottonwoods dotted the wide green lawns. Backyards sloped languidly down to the lake. I backed up the long driveway. Better to negotiate the curves now, in case I needed to make a fast get-away.

I took a deep breath before unfastening my seat belt and grabbing my camera and tripod. My hands shook.

As I shut the car door I saw Jack step off the front porch. He looked stooped, somehow. He walked with a slight limp, probably from the car accident he had months before our divorce. "Bear!" He held out his arms to hug me.

I stuck out my hand to shake his. It felt cold. "Mary," I reminded him. He smelled like laundry soap. That he didn't reek of alcohol was as startling to me as if his eyes had changed colors.

"Mary," he repeated, smiling down at me. "It's going to be hard to remember that." We walked up the drive. "Flo and Mother left for the afternoon so we could be alone. And of course Flo didn't want to see you. She still thinks of you as the 'other woman.'" He laughed.

I followed him into the coolness of the house. "She's got nothing to worry about from me." My heart pounded against the tight coldness in my chest.

We settled ourselves on pale yellow upholstered chairs. Jack leaned heavily back, but I sat straight, pressing my feet solid on the deep carpeting. I glanced quickly out towards the lake. When Bob was six he had played Star Trek in that backyard. Jack had spit in my face on that deck.

"That's new," Jack said eyeing the stars tattooed into a bracelet around my right wrist. Suddenly I remembered what he always said about women and tattoos. *Biker chicks and whores. That's what kind of a woman gets a tattoo.*

I traced my finger over it. "I've become quite the tattoo addict. This is my favorite."

Jack shook his head and grinned. "Kids." Eleven years older, he had often treated me like a child. "You brought a camera," he said.

"I want to record this momentous event." I smiled, imagining the picture I planned.

"So tell me," Jack said. "What do you do?"

"I work at a battered women's shelter. I answer the hotline, talk to the shelter residents. Mostly I do overnight shifts." I leaned back in my chair and tucked my left leg beneath me. "What about you?" I asked.

"Computers. I work at home. I don't drive anymore."

"I can't imagine you without a jeep," I said.

Jack chuckled. "I quit camping and jeeping a long time ago."

I thought about the summer after we first married, before he started drinking again. Every weekend we camped Slumgullion Pass, between Lake City and Creed, searching for the stagecoach transfer station noted on an antique map Jack had. We finally discovered it Labor Day. I still had the horseshoe I found.

"Don't you miss it?"

"Nah. Sometimes in the fall, Flo and I drive up to Estes Park to see the aspens, but that's about it."

We sat in silence, the ticking of the mantle clock measuring out the minutes. Jack stared at his hands. Lines cut deep into his face and small red veins spidered across his nose. A drunkard's face.

"How did you wind up working in a battered women's shelter?" Jack's voice jolted me out of the trance the clock's incessant ticking was putting me in. "Don't they usually want people who have experienced that sort of thing?"

I stared at him. His face flickered a superiority I had almost forgotten. That look used to convince me I was wrong. That I must have imagined his tirades, his assaults. That was the look he wore the morning he swore he hadn't pinned me down the night before and raped me as he held his hand over my mouth. "Now why would you go and make up a thing like that?" he always asked.

Suddenly I realized how strong I had been to have survived as long as I had with this man. I sensed "Bear" sitting with me and returning my feet flat to the floor, I straightened my back.

"Life with you was hell," I said, my voice even. I kept my eyes locked into his.

After some moments he looked back down at his hands. His shoulders sagged. "I spend a lot of time with AA. I try to get to a meeting every day," he said.

I felt tired all of a sudden. All the anger I had wanted to spew at Jack, the forgiveness I had hoped he would beg from me didn't matter now. I just didn't care enough about him anymore. Nobody needed to tell me my nightmares were over.

As Jack's voice droned on, I gazed out at the lake. The water rippled along the shore, its deep blue seemingly timeless. The sky leaned dark against the mountains. The aspen leaves are pale green this time of year, I thought. Tonight Bob and I will cook hot dogs over a campfire. Later we will lie against a log, and with our shoulders touching, we'll stare up at the sky and count shooting stars.

"I need to get going," I said, interrupting Jack's monologue.

"So soon?" He looked disappointed.

Jack followed me out to my car. "You didn't take your picture."

"I don't need it anymore," I said, arranging my camera and tripod in the trunk. I reached out my hand to shake his.

Jack placed his other hand around mine. "It was good to see you," he said. "I've always wondered how you were doing."

I looked at our hands. Mine had disappeared within his. I placed my left hand on top. "I wish you well, Jack."

As I coasted down the drive, I looked back at him in my rearview mirror. His mother's wide driveway seemed to swallow him up. He stared after me, his hands hanging loosely at his sides.

At Highway 34, I pointed my car towards Estes Park and cranked up my tape player. Loveland blurred out behind me as I raced to my son and the aspens.

EXCERPT FROM

Recycled

Kristin Steele

Kate's co-worker Dwayne had not said anything specifically about his brother before. All of his relatives were just called "family." Their lines of relation were largely a mystery. But he didn't talk much about his ex-wife or what he did over the weekend either, seeming to find comfort in holding things close. Kate appreciated that he didn't burden her with therapeutic ramblings, understood that desire for silence, but felt ill-prepared as she ventured into his family tree. The limited briefing she had gotten before she left was that Leo lived in a gated retirement community just outside Las Vegas. He had two dogs, in case she had allergies. And he had already said that she could stay as long as she wanted. She imagined that Leo would be a version of Dwayne, a little older, a little more tan.

When it seemed like a decent time, she checked out of the hotel and called Leo from the lobby. On the phone, he had the energy of someone who had been awake for hours and sounded nothing like the frail bird that Dwayne had characterized. Leo said the name of the place was Golden Acres. Out of context, it made Kate think about bucolic odes to rolling open spaces where those done with the rat race could split their time between the manicured golf course and cocktail dances on the terrace. But there was nothing really golden about the stretch of Nevada desert, it was pale and dusty. There certainly were acres of it. The idealized picture contained in the name made Kate giggle at the bravado of it.

She drove up to the entrance to Golden Acres and stated her name and destination as requested. The guard wore what looked like an antique police uniform, complete with white gloves, and smiled sweetly as he scanned the approved visitor list. He gave her a temporary visitor's pass and sent her through to the next wave of directional guards stationed with revolving slow and stop signs, sending cars to the appropriate lane. Everyone working looked at least seventy, silver-haired, otherworldly cheery and bright. There was nothing that indicated this might be where people went to wait to die.

As Kate drove along Main Street, she felt like she had just passed through a portal to another planet. Not only were there pink flamingos stuck at regular intervals in yards, but also the eerie smiling faces of yard gnomes peeked out of bushes and small-scale windmills turned in the light breeze. On Golden Rain Road, a woman rode a three-wheeled bicycle with a vanity plate of "Toots" surrounded by a customized frame that read, "Still Having Fun!" People power-walked along the sidewalks in chatty groups waving as she drove past at the posted ten miles an hour. She got a whistle and a thumbs up from a man presumably admiring the classic car. Kate smiled, waved back. It seemed the neighborly thing to do.

Leo lived on Cherry Blossom Lane and came out to meet Kate when she pulled into the driveway. He had closely-shorn silver hair, the hairline making an M just above his forehead. His build was thick and square, like his brother's, but seemed softer somehow in an outfit of slacks and a cardigan. His watery brown eyes focused behind thick, gold-rimmed glasses that curled behind small, red ears.

"Did you find it alright?"

"Yes, great directions."

"Come in, bring your bags, we'll get you settled."

She followed him into the towering white stucco house. Inside was a series of rooms full of stately furniture with boldly colored canvases that all looked like they were done by the same artist. One wall of the living room was eight large canvases mounted two high, four across. All were color variations on the same design—a stylized bank of color hitting a horizon and a sky of brightly colored clouds above it. It was a dreamy, bubbly landscape where the water could be burgundy, clouds a regal purple. Each frame reached out to the next creating two long horizons running the length of the long wall. She pulled away from the paintings and looked around. It was unlike any home she had put together. There were no frayed corners, no cardboard boxes or milk crates turned into makeshift furniture.

"I've got a room all set upstairs for you. Dwayne said you wouldn't want me to make a big deal out of anything. But I'm glad you're here."

"Me too," Kate smiled earnestly, though she couldn't tack down a tangible reason she would be glad to be at her co-worker's brother's house in a gated community in the middle of the desert two weeks from Thanksgiving after breaking up with her girlfriend and kicking her sister out of her house. Regardless, it was somewhere else and that she wouldn't have to tell Leo any of that if she didn't want to settled her.

The staircase came alive in a swirl of fur and tongues and feet. Two collies lurched to beat one another to the main floor where they threw their weight up onto Kate. Dancing on their hind legs, they licked and bit at her flailing arms, following her as she tried to put a piece of furniture between herself and their onslaught.

"Hey!" Leo screamed and grabbed their collars, pulling them back to a seated position on either side of him. "I'm so sorry."

Kate wiped the saliva off her forearms and let their shed fur cascade to the carpet. "Oh, it's okay."

"They're good when it's just me, but get a little excited with anyone else." He dragged the resisting dogs, nails and skidding feet across the tile kitchen floor and ushered them outside, closing the door quickly before they could reenter. "They'll mellow out in a bit." He came back into the kitchen, "I made coffee if you'd like some."

The room was a paradise of appliances assembled for a love affair with food. A rack of thick, gleaming pots and pans hung from the ceiling over the island where the granite countertop was cool under her hands. She watched Leo's deliberate movements unhindered by any of her preconceived notions about his age.

"Do you take anything in it?"

"Black is perfect." She gestured toward the front door with her thumb, "That's one beautiful car."

"Thank you for bringing it. I've missed it." He grew quiet for a moment then smiled, "Did it handle well?"

"Yes, it likes the open road."

"David loved it for that very reason."

Kate felt the tug of absence in Leo's voice. Everything indicated a pair. Matching leather swivel chairs under delicate reading lamps. Two hooks by the door for keys. Dwayne had left the *Leo is gay part out.* Avoided the detail of the dead lover. She pictured Dwayne trying to give her clues, not knowing how. His shyness about how to explain it all to her making it that not saying anything was better than him botching the attempt. But he had thought to send her there, to connect them, perhaps suspecting that it would be good for her. She had no idea that she was delivering such precious cargo with the car and was mortified at her speed and swagger in driving to Nevada.

She looked at Leo who seemed like a big man in a fragile place, and walked over to a canvas on a hunch. "Did David paint all of these?"

"Yes." Leo smiled and turned to the painting closest to him like a frozen moment in time. The framed square was a huge nest of red hatch marks resting at the very tip of a thin limb. The grass along the bottom was orange.

"How long ago did you lose him?"

"January."

"I'm sorry." She waited to feel overwhelmingly tense or awkward around this stranger whose tragedy was in the air between them, but she didn't.

"I drove up to Dwayne's after that for a while. When I was ready, he insisted I fly back and that he'd bring the car down before the holidays."

"Came in under the wire."

"Yes, thank you." He turned back from the painting, "Let me get you that coffee."

They sat in the living room on austere but comfortable couches under the wounds cleaved open by a dead painter and made small talk, an activity that Kate had never been good at. It always felt like when her family went to Aunt Gracie's for dry ham at Easter and she had to sit on the davenport and report on second grade. Leo wanted to know about how she liked her job. How Dwayne was really doing since the divorce. What she liked to do with her free time. She kept her recent inebriated carousing to herself, choosing instead to watch movies quietly at home with friends. And watching him accept these things as fact made it easier for her to try and believe them too. She could be anyone there. She could be responsible, and carefree, and solvent. She could be a joyful girl if she wanted to.

Leo let the dogs back in, and they mauled Kate again. The larger of the two settled in to humping her leg before Leo could grab hold of collars and jerk them back to good behavior. Kate got the sad impression that these dogs had been David's, too. And Leo's exhaustion with them was something he had chosen to bear.

"Are you hungry? The buffet starts soon, let an old man buy you lunch."

He looked excited and Kate nodded because she wanted him to stay that way. They sauntered out the front door and down the street in the surreal warm air. They walked over regularly spaced scores in perfect concrete winding through the maze of uniform homes toward the clubhouse. Beyond the walls of Golden Acres, the vistas opened all around them, everything the color of desert without any natural greenery to break it up. There were fluffy clouds hanging in place amid the hazy blue, barely moving. It was a model universe, where a big hand could plunk down a new tree or house at any time. Turn the lights on or off. Lay the track for a midnight train. Kate's lungs felt bigger as she inhaled the light breeze blowing across the hair on her arms.

White linens stretched across the tables, napkins folded into ornate fans peeking out of each place setting in a room full of animated personalities. They joined the line curving out the door. Kate felt out of place among the niceties, reminders of the gulf between her and Madison, between her and so much of the world. She hadn't expected that lunch would be so fancy. The food tables stretched on and on with every sort of offering imaginable. While she tried to look delicate, Kate found herself with a mounded plate barely halfway down the stretch. Leo introduced her to a blur of names she would never remember. She hadn't been hugged that much in years, if ever. While she didn't feel like she knew how to hug them back, she tried, ducking low to bring her long arms around grandmothers who'd seemingly been awaiting her arrival.

They sat among a table of Leo's friends and ate, Kate flanked by two women who talked to her about their granddaughters. They claimed she looked just like them. Her unknown doppelgangers. The lunchtime entertainment was a tuxedo-clad jazz trio in for the week from Reno. Some people got up and danced after they were done eating and wait staff cleared away the dirty plates.

"Pretty good aren't they?" Leo motioned toward the stage, tapping his foot in rhythm.

Kate smiled back at him. She looked around the room and noticed that, for a routine Wednesday lunch, no one appeared to be having anything but a grand old time. There at the edge of civilization and the great beyond between it and the nearest place, these men and women had created their very own bubble.

And she was inside it, with a full belly and sweet company and a band covering Coltrane that wasn't half bad.

Kate woke up from her lunch-induced nap barely able to breathe. The heat vent next to the bed pushed gusts of hot air into the closed bedroom. The sounds of dog sniffing ran back and forth along the bottom of the door. The hair around her face and the collar of her shirt were damp with sweat. When her pursuers took their leave, she got up, changed her shirt, and washed her face. She wandered around the quiet house until she found Leo out back watering with the dogs.

"How did you sleep?"

"Sorry, I'm not used to eating that much."

"You don't look like you eat much at all." He smiled.

A jumbo jet made its way across the clear sky, the sound separate and behind it. Kate looked at all of the magenta and orange blooms scattered around the back yard. It felt strange to see color that time of year.

"Is this normal weather?"

"A little warm for November. But us old folks like it, it's good for arthritis." He winked.

She laughed at his depiction of old, it was a word that she wouldn't use with him. "How long have you lived out here?"

"We moved in when they finished building four years ago, but we left San Francisco in 1989."

"Do you miss it?"

"Some parts, but most of it we were glad to leave. Watching everyone you know die is hard." He said it calmly, like a weather forecast.

Kate lit a cigarette. The distance of experience between them made her feel heavy. There was no response that felt adequate, no reference point. She'd only been eleven then. Taking school field trips across the Golden Gate Bridge to see *La Traviata* at the War Memorial, the subtitles barely translating the Italian tragedy enough for her and her giggling classmates. She'd never had a sense of the graveyards of living and dead she was approaching as her tour bus sped down Market, past Castro, toward the picturesque scenery of the Embarcadero.

"We've been invited to head down to the pool for a swim if you're up for it."
She nodded, the sun felt good, and she wanted to float.

The pool was a maze of slides and waterfalls that connected different
waterways all capped by a swim-up bar at the end. She followed Leo pool-
side toward a line of women sprawled out on lounge chairs, in bright ruffled
swimsuits, with piles of glossy magazines. They waved simultaneously, like a
line of windshield wipers. Kate looked down at her makeshift outfit of shorts
and an undershirt, but no one else seemed to care. She was starting to sense
the rhythms of Golden Acres, the lack of taxation within its walls, and was
ready to buy her own perfect stucco house. She sauntered over to the deep
edge and dove in, breaking the still surface to dive down, touch the bottom,
and come back up where her lungs seized and she vowed, again, to cut back
on smoking. The water was the same temperature as the air. She floated on
her back for a while, all the sounds around the pool muffled into some other
language. She watched the clouds above her morph slowly from dragon to
hot air balloon.

Over the afternoon, she talked to a rotation of people about everything.
They especially liked that she drove a recycling truck with Leo's brother,
whom they all seemed to know and have funny stories about. She didn't have
as many to tell back. They wanted to· know where she was from, didn't she
love the desert, how long was she staying, what were her favorite books, did
she have any siblings, what did her parents do. They were innocuous lines of
inquiry, but the sheer volume of them coupled with her pauses to search for
true answers made her tired. Golden Acres seemed like the kind of place she
could dream in and she had the inclination to start making up a family, to
add all the details she'd ever wished for. But sizing up what her family *was* to
make up what they *weren't* seemed like it would take as much energy, or even
more, than simply avoiding saying much about them at all.

"Only one sister?" The woman, who everyone called Lollipop, took a
long slug of jungle juice through a curly red straw, the top of the extended
umbrella knocking against the lens of her sunglasses.

Kate nodded.

"Where does she live?" Her southern drawl pushed the sentence all
together and drew out the syllable at the end.

Flashes of red from Lollipop's fingernails caught Kate's eye. "Denver."

"And what does she do there?"

95

Another in the catalog of mysteries. "I don't know."

"Well, is she married?"

Kate nodded, and picked at the callus on her hand.

"That's probably what she does then." And then Lollipop roared like a woman liberated from the chains of matrimony. Her husband was probably in her freezer.

They started a game of water volleyball. Lollipop insisted Kate play on her team and, despite all the legalities of team rotation, tried to keep Kate up at the net to block and spike the ball. "You're as tall as one and a half of us. Just slap it back at 'em." Losing at water volleyball was certainly not in Lollipop's agenda for the day.

But Kate pulled back most of the force of her returns, looking at the soft, aged faces through the net there simply to play, not to win. After a tied game that Lollipop initially argued should not be allowed to stand, everyone made their way to the pool bar while Kate took her pruned self over to the lounge chairs and lay outstretched, her closed eyelids bright with afternoon sunlight. She read gossipy magazines with large, exclamation point laden headlines and put sunscreen on her pasty limbs. Everyone was capitalizing on an unusually warm November day as if there was no difficulty anywhere. They'd left it all behind somewhere and rolled out only the greenest grass in its place. She looked over at Leo, splashing under a clear blue sky, and imagined David's paintings talking to him, calming him, giving him strength to get up in the morning.

The Visit

Victoria Wheeler

She arrived at 11:00 a.m. sharp in the Ann Arbor train station. Elizabeth May did not fly now that security people patted down travelers and expected everyone to rush to remove shoes, coat, sweater, hat and gloves needed for Midwestern cold. The train gave her the freedom to loosen her stiff joints whenever she pleased, and more importantly, no one bothered her. She had time to contemplate what she would say to her niece, Samantha, in this dead of winter.

As she stepped off the Empire Builder, she smiled at the middle aged conductor who extended his hand. "Thank you so very much," she said with a squeeze.

"Yes Ma'am," he replied as he curved his arm around her elbow and guided her out of the crush of people hurrying past. His smile revealed straight, white teeth gleaming under his graying mustache. He was handsome, the kind of man she had been attracted to decades ago. Holding eye contact with him temporarily distracted her.

Then she was alone. She remembered the reason for her journey. Icy air bit her nose.

"Aunt Elizabeth! You're here!" Samantha's younger sister, Joy, squeezed her aunt so hard that they almost fell in a heap.

"Be careful now. I'm a little unsteady in this snow. Can you get my bag?"

Joy had grown into a stunning young woman.

"You look so much like my sister." Elizabeth May's tears blurred the scene into runny blobs of color. She let her youngest niece lead her to the car with a red-mittened hand.

As Joy navigated the curves of Huron River Drive, Elizabeth stared at ten shades of gray out the car window.

Joy finally spoke. "Samantha is a wreck. She won't talk to anyone. All she does is stay home and drink. I'm so worried."

"You have good reason to be."

"I was afraid you wouldn't come. I haven't seen you since Mom's funeral." Joy gripped the wheel as the car skidded an inch or two on the frosty pavement of the first small bridge.

"I did exactly the same thing Samantha is doing after my son died. Maybe I can help."

"I hope so."

Ice pellets hit the windshield like frozen bullets as they drove across the second bridge.

winter drive, Sibelius

Hannah Thomassen

windshield wipers clearing rain,
heat/defrost taking turns, road
before me, road behind, static
on the tuner, home almost out of range,

      seek/find settles
      on symphony number three—

trees bare   branches tender
  gesture to a wet sky
                 sheep
                  like laundered pillows
                    plumped on pastures already green

        vineyard rosy brown
       valor of geese overhead

red barn   white roof
   (that wheelbarrow, those chickens in the rain)

       fields stretching to hills mounded, rounded
        held in haze fading to forever   oh if I were a painter
            it would all be about horizons

the music coming on big and important now
trucks like mountains all around
my little car fills, spills
through valleys of spray

99

Coming Clean

Diane English

It's hard work, coming clean, difficult for a woman who has lived long on our earth, who has a lot of unlearning to do. A newborn doesn't have a problem with clean. She arrives clean, direct from Nature, packaged in a fine patina shine, no problem for a mother's eyes flooded with first glance unconditional love.

Nurses in sterile hospitals have a different version of clean. They rush away with the baby, shortly after birth, rub and scrub her, poke and prick her, weigh and wrap her. Re-packaged, she's presented to mom all over again.

From that point on, a girl is expected to "put her best foot forward," especially when company comes, to come clean to birthday parties, and Sunday school. Before long coming clean is the norm. It's not just for special occasions that a girl must show up clean, but every school day for nine months a year, twelve years or more, and forever after in the workaday world. All that purification pays off when she presents herself to her husband as the epitome of clean—virgin clean.

But grunge builds and over time it gets harder and harder to get and stay clean. She becomes skilled at duplicity, discovers all kinds of tools to assist her: manners, makeup, perfume, hair dye. She masters other skills long known to womankind: hiding thoughts, suppressing feelings, disguising desires. For her efforts she's rewarded with approval from parents, teachers, bosses, and of course, her husband. She adopts others' expectations as her own, adding more layers each year until she no longer knows her natural, unsullied self.

Like an infection festering beneath a hardly noticeable plastic surgery line, the lies and shams drag her down. When she can no longer stand without assistance, she reaches out for help, rejecting family suggestions, selecting instead an unfamiliar guide...a therapist. Then, after years of hard work, months of counseling, hours of imaginary conversations with family and friends, thousands of journal pages, decades of delving into dreams, one grimy veil at a time is removed until...one day, in a mirror on the back of her bedroom door, she sees beyond her bumps and barnacles, sees through her creped skin and sagging chin and discovers she's as squeaky clean and beautiful as the moment she arrived in this world.

Sweet Youth

Marina Braun

Sweet and unfettered innocence of youth
That doesn't—not as yet—know any doubts,
Which makes it effortless to plight one's troth,
Or travel far and seek to conquer both
Parched deserts and forbidding mounts.

You never question what you see;
You boldly rush towards bright mirage;
You steer right towards a Moby Dick at sea;
You feel disdain for those who do not agree,
You feel immune from their words' barrage.

As youth retreats, as Kronos ruled it must,
The seas and deserts lose all appeal;
Despite some victories, most wars you lost;
Misgivings chase away the eyeless trust;
To guard your plans, you keep them under seal.

But white-robed Klotho keeps on spinning;
My thread has not been severed yet.
Until it happens and while I am breathing,
I crave to feel again the pounding
Of my heart; I want my clock reset.

I care not about physics of the rainbow;
I want to take a stroll along its arch;
When wandering in woods, I hear an echo,
I'll know again who's crying for her beau;
And in the sky, I'll see the gods' brave march.

My mind insists this might be a mistake;
Yes, folly it might be but I feel light and heedless;
Obeying voice of reason, I may take
A bubbling spring for a mirage, and thus forsake
The rainbow, and the woods, and precious oneness.

There's no going back, I'm ready to traverse
Anew the arid desert, searching for oasis;
My map is all my life's events, both fair and adverse,
While you, my troubadour, romantic verse,
Your voice, your eyes, your hands—my compass.

Street Kid

Doris Hammons

Livin on the street
ain't so easy.
You get cold stares, cold hands and
cold, cold feet.
Can't get no meals, can't get no work
can't get a drink
can't feel safe, can't keep clean.

Tell the boss, "Part time don't cut it,"
He smiles and says he'll do something about it.

Just when I think can't be no worse,
all I own is stolen by some jerk.

Hate to ask Grandma, really takes me to task,
then it's off to the Thrift Store we go
to buy me some new used clothes,
man, oh man, I'm feeling low.

Washed my bod, found a second job.
I guess my luck is looking up.
I'll work real hard, I won't be beat.
I can't forget those cold, cold streets, cold
stares, cold hands, cold, cold feet.
It's a slice of hell livin' on the street.

The Guest

Frances Kiva

A slow, gentle guest creeps in through my back door that I can never latch tightly no matter what I try. Quietly, the guest looks around my house and finding it hospitable, stays.

The guest keeps very still and out of my way at first, but feeling ignored he begins to make his presence known. Just little things; like leaving a white hair in my brush, or sneaking into my room when I'm sleeping and wrinkling my sheets so that when I wake in the morning my face is lined. He exchanges all my books so I can only see the print at arm's length. He steepens my stairs, so I can no longer run from my basement to my third-floor attic bedroom.

Affectionate, my guest touches me, prodding all my old injuries so that they reawaken and repay me for turning my bike too fast or trying to ride an untrained horse. His touch, like a lover's, strays into new territory, brushing my knuckles, my knees, my neck which in response become stiff and sore and hard to bend.

He plays with my thermostat, making my house alternately freezing and sweltering until my body is thrown so out of whack that even my dependable monthly cycle ceases. He turns down the volume on my stereo, on my television, and everything else he can find, until all becomes muted. He changes my light bulbs so at night it is never bright enough. He serves me taffy and my teeth loosen. Always a trickster, he hides things—my keys, my wallet, and even changes the streets so that I get lost in the city I have lived in for most of my life.

At times I tire of him and try to find ways to make him leave. I try new diets rich in fruits and vegetables, whole grains, and lean protein that I think he doesn't like. One by one, I cut out tobacco, over-drinking, and late night parties, hoping to bore him. I make him join me in strict exercise routines. I drag him to spas, religious ceremonies, and doctor's offices. Nothing works. He stays.

As our relationship deepens, he becomes jealous. I'm not sure how he does it but he drives the people in my life away. First, my beloved Grandmum stops visiting and calling, moving so far away I can only contact her in my memories, then he starts on my parents, and then their siblings, and finally, my friends and lovers, until my world is more populated with people that used to be than are.

Finally, when the guest has explored every inch of my house, he invites me to come to his. At first, I put him off. I have things I need to do. My garden needs tending. My dog needs walking. My granddaughter is graduating and needs to have the party at my house. But finally, he insists; I would be rude to keep him waiting any longer. So one day we leave my house, hand in hand, latching the door behind us.

Job Hunting in the New Information Age

Barbara E. Berger

Dear Head Recruiter of Information-Age Workers, Inc.:

Thank you for taking me on as a client. As we discussed, I have eleven years experience as a freelancer. I am now interested in a permanent, full-time position in a creative think tank or a research firm. My skills include translating, writing, investigating and forecasting.

Here is a brief history of my own efforts to find full-time work in the last year. I have also enclosed information about my freelance research project accomplishments. At first, I had spotty results from posting my resume on the Internet: "aspiring psychic seeks day job as newspaper columnist." One announcement I received read: "Wanted: obituary writer for weekly community newspaper." The job requirements included writing obituaries to accompany the newborns announced in their "births" column. The obituaries would foretell the future accomplishments of the infants, describing their impressive impacts on society in the decades to come and listing the loved ones they would leave behind. Out of sensitivity to the new parents, the paper would withhold the future date of the newborns' deaths.

I had reservations. What if the child was to become a criminal? A bank robber. A rapist. A defector. Or, a test subject for making ethical choices without an emotional guidance system or conscience. Those studies are already under way; did you know that? They will need more subjects. Or, what if the child was a torturer of small insects or of large land mammals? Perhaps of small insects ON large land mammals? Or, the child eventually died alone, unloved and unnoticed due to an incurable introversion and agoraphobia that trapped the poor creature in a lifetime of solitude and nothingness.

I passed on this job. Why break hearts before their time?

I reposted my resume, this time focusing on my multi-lingual talents. My resume bragged, "Writer and translator, freelance. No project too big or too small. Specializes in working with obscure and dead languages. (Real-time channeling services available at extra charge.)"

The following project proposals quickly filled my e-mail inbox.

Proposal 1. Please tell me what my mother meant when she said on her death bed, "I'll come back and make you sorry you were ever born." Are any of my dead-end relationships with narcissistic, self-absorbed "metro-sexuals" examples of her threat coming true? (This one I took on. But the proposer still doesn't believe my answer: "yes." Hey, don't knock it. What would *you* say?)

Proposal 2. I will pay you $10,000 for every essay you write revealing the secrets of until-then unsolvable crimes. Bonus if a television station picks one up as a pilot. Secrets must be verifiable, preferably in the form of an authentic confession. (This one, though very tempting, I passed on. Would have to turn in my sources—that would be breach of ethics and trust.)

Proposal 3. Every morning at 10:00 a.m. the clouds arrange themselves to give me a special message of the day. But, lately, I have not been reading them accurately. I used to be able to get winning lottery numbers. Now, seems all I get are locations of the best sales on laundry detergent. Could you talk to the clouds? Get them back on task? (I am still investigating this one. Not sure if the clouds are off task, or if they are punishing the proposer passive-aggressively, or if the proposer simply lost his code book.)

The word got out that I was reliable and I had more work than I could hope to get. However, they were still one-time assignments. My portfolio has some samples of work I am most proud of. Please see enclosures for the executive summaries of the research I conducted. In all cases, my methodology is trade secret and not available. Pragmatic results provide verification for accuracy.

Enclosure 1. Amazon River Project. On this assignment, my team and I deciphered twelve secret languages of blue- and purple-colored birds in the Amazon River Delta. Sample phrases and their English meanings appear in the summary. Optional CD of bird dialogue and prayer meetings recorded in the field are available on request.

Enclosure 2. Human Infant Cry Project. Conducted independent research and wrote a codebook for parents. The codebook translates into English the nuances of 45 varieties of infant cries. Bonus appendix: sighs, gurgles, and burps. Special section on midnight-hour screeches and coos at dawn. In the accompanying CD, adult humans imitate the infants in order to protect their anonymity.

Enclosure 3. Human Body Language Made Audible. Translated 316 most common illicit flirtations. Produced computer program which will translate suspected flirtations in real time. Plug in the earphones, and hear what everyone at the party, in the office, or in the park is saying with their body. Based on the five most common dialects in the eastern United States. English dialects of San Francisco underclass; Portland, Oregon street people; New York City South Pier longshoreman; Manhattan East 80's; and other special requests currently being studied and programs written.

Enclosure 4. Burned Diary Recovery Project. Have completed 16 text recoveries of diaries burned in rage, fear and self-denial. Due to its public service nature, I plan to continue to provide these services even when employed full-time. Requires diary author to be alive. (For now.)

As you can see, I have been innovative in applying my skills to a variety of projects. I believe I would be a valuable member of any creative team, or a skillful leader of a team. Please let me know of any firms that could use my writing, forecasting, researching, and project management skills on a permanent, full-time basis. I prefer to work for the common good in an organization that has good health care benefits (including mental health). I am willing to relocate, but prefer to live as far away as possible from my personal vortex of evil (will share its location if offered a position in its vicinity).

Sincerely,
Job Seeker in the New Information Age
Encls.

The City of Dead Languages

Heidi Schmaltz

Past

These are the languages the first people spoke
The language that did or did not enter through the Bering Straight
The language that comes from here
The language buried in the eruption of Mt. Mazama
The language that crossed the Bridge of the Gods
The language spoken by WyEast and LooWit
In ash clouds
The language that found Lewis and Clark
The language that holds the history in between
A language that has been fished with for 15,000 years
A language that gathered huckleberries, wapato

Most of us are strangers to his landscape
We live here
Lost in infinite translation

Which Oregon are you from?
In my Oregon they haven't always spoken English
My Oregon publishes in German
In Oregon, many a Thanksgiving dinner has been conducted in Swedish
In my Oregon people speak Russian and Tongan
Turkish and Laotian.
The Tongan kids born here learn dances
That could row them across the Pacific
In ritual

The old Vietnamese men
Haven't learned English
But will test out their French with you

The Cubans speak Russian
And the Cuban *santos* who walk down Glisan in white
Speak Lucumi as well

My grandmother,
Upon learning that our waiter at Timberline lodge was Norwegian
Began to sing the national anthem
With such pride
We have diaries of sea voyages in this language
In our attic
And little sayings hanging in the kitchen

We all have other languages
In boxes in our attics
Or at least on holidays
Is this your Oregon too?

Present

Portland is a mass of new faces
Transforming it, hiding history
The new facade is pleasing
As polished as the Pearl
That neighborhood is rough underneath
It used to be called Old Town
Where you can still find the old languages
Passed out drunk in the doorways
And our liberal love of diversity
Is absent in the places
Where the people of color live
And how Gresham has become the new ghetto

Portland is the place
Our grandparents learned English
The place they slowly forgot their mother tongues
A place of genocide
The city of dead languages

North Boneville in October
The Indians have smoked fish hanging up in the trees
Bones, heads, and tails
No meat

They live there, by the river
In shelters made of tarps and plywood
An occasional trailer with a plywood door
Tarp window
They speak English with a hint of an accent
Barely hanging on
Barely hanging there
Like the fish in the trees
Bones with the meat scraped off

Future

 What if Spanish was no longer spoken here?
And had diluted into diglossia
And the children of Honduras
Of Mexico
Of El Salvador
Wandered the streets looking for words?
Spanish is no longer spoken here
And the power of the language of Columbus
The language learned by La Malinche
And interpreted for 500 years
Is unable to express itself
Inside the required grammatical structures
And the English-only classrooms

This silence brings a world without words
Without speech
Without meaning

What languages will be welcome in this world?
Will we confine them geographically?
Will they end up on reservations and in bad neighborhoods?
Will we put them behind barbed wire?

Will we become unable to describe this horror?
Unable to look at things in different ways?
Unable to see ourselves,
Unable to reason?
Will we tell our grandchildren
That we don't know our own language?

I want them to speak a language
That isn't domination
I want a world
Made by the word
I want a world
In many languages
I want a world
Interpreted through love

I see
Resurrection through concrete
The old languages coming back
New words
Blossoming—
Flowers,
New life
In a once dead land.

Dreaming
You

mapping a bare country

Dreaming You While Driving the Columbia – for Alice

Kristin Berger

Down from arid wheat land
a black basalt ridge seams
the world together.
Bunch-grass shoulders
the soft earth that slopes,
with an ancient arching,
to the river. Windsurfers skid—
damselflies winging
a brittle brilliance across
wide water, for each other.

Against my weathered and slumped bones,
you rest. Your spine rocks within.
Lovely pearls, strung in sleep
mapping a bare country,
a pure calcifying will
strengthening under the moon's
pale belly pressed
against a taut, empty blue.
You crave to crest
into your first breath,

from gill to wing
in one ambitious flip
below the cage of my ribs.

Together we skirt cliff-bottoms,
speed with metallic grace
as lasting as our wake
along the black backbone of beginning,
holding river currents
to their course,
towards the mouth
and the bar's eventual unraveling.

In the Tenth Month

Kristin Berger

Most everything is clear.
The night's moon halves
between fir limb and roof pitch
a blue pool spilling
into the steel sink, a shine
that out-weighs street lamps
and my own turning on.

Midnight rivers and their tributaries
spider down my breasts, down
mountain of baby
covered in parchment,
submerged turtle shell,
to the shadows carried
in the moment's underbelly.

The white kimono
inked in indigo flowers
no longer closes,
the sash atop my ribs
tail of comet
loose end of the script
still spooling over
the page, the quill quivering
before dawn floods
the bearable dark.

Love as a Verb

Gerri Ravyn Stanfield

Eleven o'clock on the bedside alarm and my eyelids sank as my partner, Michael rehearsed his presentation for work. I listened tolerantly and disguised my yawn. "You'll be brilliant. I've got your back"

"Thanks, but what does that mean?"

I turned on my side to survey him. "I don't know exactly—we used to say it in Kentucky. It's like saying I support you, I love you, don't worry about a thing."

"It kind of implies a threat, doesn't it?"

"What do you mean?"

"Well, you wouldn't have to defend someone's back unless they were in danger, right?"

"I guess so. I never pondered the philosophy." His kiss grazed my cheek and he stretched to darken the lamp.

The first time my family left Kentucky on a vacation that didn't involve piling into our old Buick to visit my grandparents happened when my father won a trip to Disneyworld for selling the most air filters. He was proud of not having to wear a uniform to work anymore and determined to show his family how the other half lived. We rode on an airplane and I left grooves in the arm rests with terrified eleven year old fingernails. My mother asked for extra complimentary peanuts and saved them in her brand new Liz Claiborne purse so that we had snacks for the amusement park. My little brother, Trey and I stuffed ourselves with ice cream sandwiches shaped like Mickey Mouse. For the first time, we stayed in a real hotel with luxurious white towels. We waited in line in the swampy Florida humidity to get our picture taken with Goofy. I pouted because I was too old for Disneyworld and my cut offs were too short and my shirts weren't fitting right because I had outgrown them all. I kept thinking about the kids at school and how I might get an allowance or even a ten speed bike and ride to the dollar movies by myself. My parents fought incessantly at the park; my mom clutched her new purse and tried to convince my dad not to spend so much money on games and beer. Afterward, we arrived late at the Orlando airport and there was a last minute gate change so we ran and ran. They wouldn't let us on the plane home even though it was parked at the gate taunting us. My father's voice began to swell and a royal violet flush spread across his neck. The woman behind the counter was shrinking and my mom was saying "Luke, calm down, don't make a fuss" with a hand on his arm and apologizing for him and he was shaking her hand away like a dish towel. Soundlessly, Trey and I reversed our steps, pretending we did not belong to this strange loud man. I held my brother's hand, keeping him to my left, consciously placing myself between him and my father. His hand was stained and sticky from the ice cream and he whispered "shit" as my father drop kicked our luggage across the airport, each kick punctuated by obscenities that I was sure had never been heard in Florida before.

In the early years of high school, my friends and I used to party in our buddies' basement, dubbed the Chicken House for reasons no one remembered. We purchased alcohol from Ron, the 21-year-old brother of our friend Angus, who worked at the convenience store down the street. We could drink freely at the Chicken House and the cops were rarely called. There was always too much else going on around our side of town to occupy police attention. There weren't enough teenagers in Louisville to make more than one counter-culture scene so we felt obligated to share these hangouts, as well as the local alternative music store. It was an uneasy collision of outcasts: the punks, the stoners, the cowboys from the East side and occasionally, a random bunch of skinheads whom no one could abide for very long. I hated it when they showed up because I inevitably argued with them over racist comments to no avail and everyone teased me about my bleeding heart. We clustered together and chain smoked cigarettes surrounded by the bizarre bedfellows of combat boots, skateboards, tie dyed t-shirts, Mohawks, western hats and red plastic cups of beer. The music invaded us, offering the invitation to become revolutionary or at least, relevant. The stereo created a perpetual source of conflict.

As the hours became saturated with liquor, fights erupted. One night, one of the skinheads pulled a gun when Angus snatched his cassette from the stereo and tossed it out the door. We all scattered, our cups suddenly airborne. I crouched beside the washing machine with Carl in his worn leather jacket who shielded me with his body. I loved Carl best because he didn't say *ain't* as much as the other guys and he brought me McDonald's hamburgers when he got off work. He knew but never mentioned that there wasn't much food in my house since my dad had left and my mom was working two jobs. His taut neck smelled of fear and French fry grease and I willed us both to be invisible. My best friend, Melina, was frozen on the couch in the middle of the basement, repeating in a slurred voice "I can't believe I'm friends with you people". She remained there, statuesque and unaffected while Angus and the skin head bellowed at each other and the gun became a pendulum pointing in every direction. We beckoned with furious hand signals for her to duck and crawl over to us but she stared straight ahead. I wondered crazily how surreal the gun was to Melina, who did not live in our neighborhood. Her parents owned a six bedroom house in the Highlands and I often thought her life was all about bluegrass, horse races and mint juleps. Her family sat down to dinner together every night and went to Hilton Head every summer. As far as I knew, she had never seen anything like this before except in the movies. In that moment, the gun was the most authentic thing in the room. It was the only pertinent element in my world, a twisted tool of divination. If that gun spoke, would I ever write?

Would I get the hell out of this town? Would it always be like this? I gripped Carl and waited unobtrusively to see if the steel fortune teller would articulate anyone's fate.

Tony, the 35-year-old night manager at Mr. Gatti's Pizza, harangued me because I wouldn't go out with him. He enjoyed tossing the cash register keys at me and laughing when I had to bend over to retrieve them. Because five different guys came to pick me up after work, he called me a slut and asked me which one was my boyfriend. In truth, none of them was my boyfriend; they were my best friends who had raised me and emotionally pulled me through four years of high school. A year ago, they had packed my belongings in their cars and driven me the seventy miles to the University of Kentucky. Since I was the only one of us to have gone to college, they were delighted that I was in town for the summer and we hung out together after I left the restaurant most evenings. I had complained about Tony to the general manager who told me that Tony was next in line to take over that store location and suggested that I just ask him to stop bothering me. After that, I strategically avoided interactions with him if I could. Tony acted as if his wanting to date me was a joke, but I always noticed him watching me when I mopped the floor at closing time. Of course he had angry pimples, twitchy hands, rodent features and drove a shiny black El Camino. I thought of him as an irritation rather than a predator until the night I went to put the pizza dough back in the lock-in freezer and he stood against the outside of the door and wouldn't let me out for a tense few minutes. I contemplated whether or not freezing to death would be painful and when he finally released me, I locked myself in the women's restroom, shaking and blowing on my hands. I told Carl and David about Tony over a beer the next night and they grew thundercloud silent. Immediately suspicious of their reaction, I begged them not to do anything, made them promise that they wouldn't make me lose this job. I knew my scholarship wouldn't cover my living expenses, and I had to get back to school no matter what I had to endure. They wanted to know why I hadn't come to them before now. Didn't I believe that they had my back? I asserted that I could take care of myself and didn't need their redneck brand of justice. Both promised reluctantly that they would do nothing to fix my problem and we dropped the subject. Tony showed up at work in the morning with his car window taped with plastic. He told the general manager that the window was probably vandalized by neighborhood kids. He didn't speak to me for the rest of the summer and I was able to mop under the pizza buffet in peace. I remained unaware of exactly what had changed until David confessed to me after another year had passed. On the night after my fateful beer with David and Carl, my friends were waiting for Tony after he closed the restaurant and cornered him in the parking lot. They smashed the El Camino's side window with a wooden Louisville Slugger baseball bat. They told him that all five of them were dating me and that if he didn't leave me alone, next time, they would smash his rat face. When I heard the story, I was appalled. David defended their actions by swearing to me that guys like Tony didn't believe in feminism or strong women. He told me that they all knew

I could take care of myself, but they wanted to speak to Tony in a language that he could understand, a language I would never speak.

TJ answered the door, his gangly giant frame towering over us. I was on crutches from twisting my ankle the week before. Loralee stood next to me, a fierce five feet, two inches without the hair sprayed bangs. I pointed my finger directly at TJ's chin and told him that I knew what he did to Betsy, I would tell everyone and he would never get a date again. I swore that when Loralee and I were through, every woman on campus would be whispering when he walked by and recognize him for the sick abusive freak that he was. My finger was still trembling after we had washed Betsy's indigo bruised eye and split cheekbone and allowed her to weep on our sofa bed. TJ believed he was justified in teaching his girl a lesson when other guys were looking at her. He had pronounced her skirt too short, her lipstick too bright and he needed to take her down a notch. Now, he retreated before my finger as I screeched, equalizing the size difference between us with the quantity of my voice. The neighbors were opening their doors to investigate the noise, TJ backed up, unsure of what I would do. There was power there, and vengeance. For a moment, it didn't matter that he would become violent with someone else or maybe even Betsy. He eventually found his speech to demand that I shut up but I shouted him down. I told him that he should be ashamed of himself and demanded to know what his mother would think about him right now. Invoking the Great Mother of southern culture was effective and he recoiled into his apartment. I leaned on the crutches, barely registering my swollen ankle. Loralee and I attempted to storm out, but my injury spoiled some of the effect. We hit three university bars to write "TJ Dawes beats the shit out of women" in black permanent marker in the bathroom stalls. We swore to each other that there was not one single thing we would miss about Kentucky after we graduated from college. We drove back to our apartment, high on righteousness and periodically checking the rear view mirror.

It was 11:30 p.m. when I reached for Michael in the dark "You still awake?"

"Mmmmhmmm, what's up?"

Suddenly, I wanted to tell him that growing up in working class Kentucky had taught me that love was not an associate of pacifism. Although escaping probably saved my life, I would never forget theh loyalty, the protective instinct, the kind of love that shields. Sometimes as a transplant to the west coast, I didn't know how to behave in lieu of the urgency that brings something more subterranean than love, something that can't be understood unless it is lived. Sometimes I felt like a veteran, seared and sheltered, who had been able to travel to the edge and back and hold the hands of those who went there too. Was it love that got us out alive?

It had taken me years to realize that "I love you" was as opaque and muddy as the Ohio River and people didn't all mean the same thing when they said it. Love was relative to the effort that someone was willing to put into another human. Some people expressed love as a wish for well being; it did not imply action. Love alone did not necessarily equate the willingness to fight for someone. If you loved someone, you might not want her to fall. If your feelings ran deeper, you would sweat and maybe risk your own life to pull him away from the edge of the cliff. The words, "I love you" were the pale sister of the words "I've got your back". My kind of love would always be more verb than noun.

I touched the side of Michael's face with the tips of my fingers. "I do have your back. Good luck with your presentation. Call me and tell me how it goes."

Txt msg+tech+BF=OMG modrn luv

Stacy Carleton

There I was, furiously punching away on my tiny keypad, periodically checking the cobblestone sidewalk to avoid the ubiquitous dog feces as I walked. Or stomped, rather. I seethed. I sent. Then I waited for the next msg to be lobbed back.

This, unfortunately, was my love life. It all started out innocently enough. I'd been living in Spain for a few months, where citizens, for the most part, have not embraced pooper-scoopers—hence the daily defecation side-step. I was working at an ESL teacher training school and met a charming British man on holiday with his father. After pity-partying my way through Christmas, I watched stylishly clad Spanish families walk the narrow streets to an endless soundtrack of church bells, he was a welcome distraction, breaking up my loneliness and anxiety with a constant smile and baffling phrases such as "slagging off," "silly git," and "bloody (fill in with endlessly various nouns)." We laughed all the time, and he made sure to constantly tell me just how much he adored me.

He'd look at me from across a room, and we'd both freeze, arrested in giddy, early love, our hormone-and neurochemical-addled brains bubbling over with exhilaration. During the weeks we spent together before his return to England, he betrayed his hopelessly romantic core, pulling me on elevators for furtive, heady make-outs, slipping notes that professed his infatuation with me inside the piles of papers on my desk. I was falling for him. And I tried my hardest not to, because he didn't even live in the same country.

Having never believed in long-distance relationships, I went against my better judgment and embarked on what would soon become an endless communiqué between Spain and England. Distance was built into our courtship from the start. I slaved away in my office in Sevilla, while he scootered his way through London. He visited every few weeks, but face-time was a luxury.

The relationship subsisted through phone calls, emails, and text and instant messaging. In an instantaneous moment, the "we" of our relationship was not limited to he and I. When things eventually (spoiler alert!) got ugly, our heated exchanges were all the more heightened by the presence of IM and its nosy cohorts, like smug stenographers all too pleased to translate and transfer the venom.

The totalitarian tendencies of technology presented constant looming expectations, that ball-and-chain, catch-22 of convenience. Cell phones and computers were always a lurking presence, weighty with the menacing reminder, "Your thoughts and feelings will be transmitted through us. You have no excuse for not communicating, because you are obligingly connected, all the time."

I began to enviously regard the droll predictability of the daily routines that most couples lamented. What I would have given for an unadulterated chat on the couch, our thoughts and words simply hanging in the air. Not needing to be digitized and pixelated to come into being. Our infrequent rendezvous felt desperate. The joy of simply sitting at a café table together was always undermined by the threat of our inevitable separation, when our utterances would revert to their electronic state.

Boyfriend (BF) was pretty deft at texting, and chided me for taking so long to reply and for only using 30 characters when I had 140 at my disposal. Mind you, this man was 35 years old. It was like having a techno-happy teenager at my elbow, constantly bemoaning my lack of digital finesse. BF peppered his messages with what I now recognize as insidious txt language. U wud have been amazd to c it.

The first time he said he loved me was in the form of a text message, and there was something about that that I just couldn't take seriously. Adults don't express their emotions through a shorthand language dominated by adolescents. Love is too big for that.

I had a hard time accepting luv, and all of its attendant manifestations and conflicts, on a tiny phone held in my palm. Shakespeare may have structured and reconciled the messy enormity of love within the confines of sonnet form. But BF's expectation of me to encapsulate my feelings through a piece of Nokia-issued plastic was like being asked to share my innermost desires through Morse code.

The collision of both of our intense personalities produced spectacular sparks, but, like most powerful combinations, the potency soon became a destructive force, crushing every bit of goodwill in its path. His passionate personality gave way to an underlying layer of insecurity and jealousy, which provoked a string of battles. Our fighting soon caught up with, and then overtook, our initial bliss.

Our fights navigated through and across all forums: instant messenger, email, text messages. Email and texting have a time-delay factor, which led me to punch out a rage-fueled response that resulted in a scrap of the original long-winded lament I'd intended. These limitations enraged me further. I could not abide by my fights becoming Verizon's commodity. They were making five cents on every volley and comeback.

If you've never conducted a fight via txt msgs, try your best to keep it that way. This relationship was my first experience with text wars. They were the worst kind of fights, because the exchanges were bite-sized. He would make some infuriating comment, and I, enraged, would have to respond. In 140 characters or less. Or in multi-message, where you have too much to say and the whole thing gets split up into smaller messages sent in succession to the recipient. This results in a disorder and lack of continuity that the recipient must remedy by reading the first message last. I couldn't even depend on linearity in my conflicts anymore.

Typing skills also present a problem. In one tender conversation, BF told me to fuck oof. Then to fuck off. Damn Messenger.

Instant messenger evokes the same kind of aversion that Match.com does, for its role in the commodified systemization of compatibility. I like my life organized: I keep an obsessive planner, I sort files and clothing to establish a sense of order within the scheme of the universe that leaves me panicked.

But love? Love isn't meant for charts and graphs. I recoil at the thought of feeding my romantic stats into some number-crunching program so that a pasty, pudgy Econ flunky can direct me to my betrothed. I cling to the romantic within, the poor soul constantly on the verge of being drowned by the more powerful and vocal cynic who monopolizes my psyche.

I don't want external applications of structure in my love life. I hate the idea of subscribing to planned problem-solving sessions and communication strategies, just as I hate those self-improvement books that reduce life and the self to a few simple steps, a few "Rules." Ugh. Messenger is yet another instrument in the unfortunate technologification of love.

Messenger does have its benefits, I suppose. Because it is basically a transcription of a romantic/emotional exchange, it is a transcription of the relationship. Whenever I think of visiting a new therapist and having to somehow encapsulate my existence and all of its attendant problems and people within neat verbal explanations, Messenger could be quite handy. If BF and I had ever made it to therapy, the lucky professional, with a brief perusal, could have a solid record of our highs and lows, a nice overview of our dysfunction, right there on paper. It's like having a personal scribe record every detailed exchange of emotion. Every cruel jab, every hyperbolic declaration documented. Oh, the convenience.

The deal-breaker should have been that my BF wrote everything as a text message, complete with "u," "b4," and other hideous configurations. This included handwritten notes and cards, and I recoiled every time I received one.

I'm even a grammar descriptivist, so I make lenient concessions for language misuse and innovation. I'm a firm believer in the true democracy of language, the power of the masses in language evolution. But I'd rather continue my selective linguistic snobbery than wrap my mind around a reality in which it is acceptable for adults to write this way. There is a creepy juvenile reversion about it. I can't take seriously "I luv u" written in a card. The medium is the message, and the medium privileges convenience over poetics.

The worst part was when I received a card from the BF, in which he said, "U are special. I luv u 2…." Did I say this was a hand-written card? As in, regular English forms would be called for? I'm sure he must have known how to write in standard language, but I never saw it. He was intelligent; not the most literary of the bunch, but I think he knew better. Yet he always wrote this way.

In college, one of my linguistics professors explained that anthropological studies in recent decades had been producing a growing body of evidence for the complex communication systems of apes. Still, one of the remaining distinctions within humans' one percent of genetic difference remains our ability to transmit messages from one physical setting to another. However, as our reliance on these distant communications increases, I wonder about their viability as a substitute for communication in its more basic, primal form.

The enterprise of modern technological communication relies upon a sort of suspension of disbelief—a chosen denial and acceptance of the virtual for the real. Virtual communication is just that—virtual. I would never want to think that technology-aided communication could ever truly replace the intimacy of the immediate.

Perhaps that is why I still harbor a sense of incompleteness after BF and I broke up, fittingly and for the last time, over email. Maybe it's because tears are still organic and an aching heart can't be digitized. And even if we someday find a way to fully technologize emotion, I'll still take old-school love, in all its low-tech glory, any day.

My Husband Grows Orchids

Carol Ellis

Their virginal faces turn to watch.
They lean gracefully above our disorder,
the cluttered living room, the unkept promises.

In the backyard their small, wild cousins lift in fall
under fir trees, delicate pink faces, orchids in miniature
that grow from leaf mold and piled needles.

He's always been a careful man, keeper of secrets.
His big hands, cautious with small things, move
like patient animals to tend the strict white blooms.

Family Walk at Bishop's Close

Amy Minato

Huddled together, tilted
over the shadowed pond we strain to see
pale bodies twining in a fisted knot
in the dusk-dark water.

Four salamanders curl
into each other whirling
tails whipping, fingers laced
spinning in rhythmic orbit.

Is it conflict or intimacy
that causes them to gather
nudge and coil their soft bellies
together in that cold well?

Maybe the fear of weasel-teeth,
heron-beak, the frigid water
or just the dark coming on
sends them spiraling over the muck
like Medusa or a dervish
leaving a froth of prayer.

And what compels the children
to wiggle into our bed
curve between us in their sleep
pressing skin-to-skin
limb-to-limb until dawn?

We bow low over the reflection
of our four faces, rippling
overlapping like folded hands.

A Day at Home

Amy Minato

Branch shadows on the fence
say my number is up.
Blue-cold winter dusk,
the children will soon be home.

How did I neglect
to crunch over frost-crisp grass,
tilt my face for a shower of sun?
How could I insult this day
by spending so much of it inside?

I rustled through old files,
put water out for birds
oiled squeaky bikes, cleaned
wayward dishes. But what about

the gallop of spirit, beckon
of contemplation or seductive
meander in a sunlit wood?

I meant to write a poem today
about how our sweet lives
are plucked away in tiny cottony bits
and melted on tongues of obligation.

All the while light
seduces the green world
wind gathers and arranges
hands us back to ourselves
as astonished bouquets.

Dee Highway Revisited

Amy Gray

We weren't supposed to know about the maggots. Mom didn't think we knew but we did. Nick and I both understood that it's not something that she would have shared with us. We were to learn about death the weird way, I guess. When we dug up the box and the tiny grave we thought we would see that pearly pink skin and those tiny eye-sealed faces all in a row on the ripped red velvet from the pockets of my Sunday dress. The careful way we had placed them on that precious material, how my hand could touch my leg now and no one would ever know. How we had petted the cold little skins.

Curiosity drove us. We just wanted to see them again.

I led us to the grave marked with a mossy-barked stick and a pile of rocks. We dug the hole again. When we were wild, near the creek or the cat-tails, catching crawdads with chicken bones or watching baby birds cry in their nests, my brother Nick was always first, always in front. Even though I was older, even though I was bigger, he was the leader. I wanted him more than he wanted me.

But this time I reached in, with my longer arms elbowing him back, I wanted to see them first. I pulled the box to us, we pressed cheek to cheek. I tipped the lid to the white rice-sized bodies swarming madly.

With cheeks flaming red, fascinated, we looked away and back. It was like watching barn cats having sex, the female screaming and fighting. Wanting to drop the box and run, but unable to. Together we saw the flesh of bodies without spirits eaten by tiny wiggling flies and worms. Torn open, headless. Dead.

It was a secret, the grave digging, "but if God hadn't wanted us to know he wouldn't have shown us," I said. Nick shrugged. As we trudged home at dusk we decided not to tell. It would not be a good idea for brother Pete to know, even though in time we would tell him in grizzly detail. In time we would punish him before sleep with nightmarish recollections of everything that had ever scared us, but for now he was only three years old. Mom's little baby.

We walked slowly, perusing the cattails, thick with countless nest-fulls of hungry crying naked beaks with beady black eyes. All at head level. When the screeching mama swamp birds dive-bombed us out of the bog, into the fields, we ran laughing and terrified through hay bales, home.

Like any other summer evening we bathed in warm water and gritted our teeth against the sting of grass cuts on our legs and arms. The water and soap irritating them so they shone on our skin like tiny red roadmaps, the paths of our afternoon. When a bubble stuck to his arm Nick screamed out and flicked it off, for an instant it looked like a maggot.

Days pressed into weeks and weeks into years, Nick found sports and I found books. Nick found trucks and I found out chickens eat fat garden bugs. Nick found teams and I found friends. He liked having a coach, a captain, an organized game with rules, whistles and regulations.

I liked cowboys and Indians, building tree forts, finding broken things in burned-out shacks.

Nick got a basketball hoop, games were cut and dried. I started taking more of an interest in the home life of ants and snakes.

Nick and I went to the same high school for two years. I don't remember seeing him there. I do remember when he was addicted to Weird Al Yankovic and that was the only thing he would listen to, for hours on end. Song after song after song. When mom was ripping out her hair he would put Weird Al on his headset, but I could still hear it turned all the way up and blasting out the sides.

We would band together, mom and I, each screaming from a different part of the double-wide trailer we lived in, "turn it off!" The walls were paper sheets, made to look like wood, but fake and thin. Into the walkman the tape would go—Nick's bobbing head enough motion to shake the floors.

After Weird Al he got obsessed with Hank Williams Jr. It drummed into my room through those walls. The walls were good for pretending to be a ghost and knocking at random hours into his room. I would snore lightly then feign shock and fear when he came to my bed and shook me awake, "*It's knocking again.*"

The walls were bad if you didn't want to know when your sibling has nightmares. Good if you taught each other a secret language of scratches to particular rhythms and it drowned out parents fighting, doors slamming, and numbed you to sleep.

They're terribly thin if you sneak your boyfriend in through the window and get lost touching secret mysterious places in the night.

Nick idolized Hank Williams Jr. Mom screamed, "He needs a role model!"

"He's looking for a man...." She would cry, dad would leave again to drive long-haul trucks, back to Atlanta maybe, hopefully not through Vegas.

"I'm glad you switched to Hank Williams instead of Weird Al," I told him. We were sitting on my bunk bed doing homework. Listening to a song about some woman in Cutbank, Montana, the deep husky voice similar to the one Nick would adopt years later.

"Why?" he asked.

"Because if this were a song by Weird Al it would be about cutting a banana." We laughed.

Sitting and watching clouds move in, there are still times I half-wonder if he will show up at my door, ask me to go on a hike with him to the creek, past the cattails like we used to, looking for feathers, for fur. He never has, but that doesn't mean he couldn't.

Caring for Father

Heidi Schulman Greenwald

She strokes stitches on his abdomen, a trail
traversing ribs that wraps around his back.
Outside, two men ply his yard, pointed shovels
digging trenches. They skirt lilies, yellow buds
still lingering. Lavender unearthed, roots to sky.
She inquires. Leak in the sprinkler system,
one man replies. He checks irrigation pipes, she thinks
knife through skin, gliding past intestine, skirting
riven lower rib, liver, to staunch bleeding. I've got it.
She looks up sees the second man, a faint spray before
his face. The men heave clay to trenches, tamp
lavender back home. One branch buried under earth.

Collision of Love

A Haibun for 2002

Wendy Thompson

I write my riddles
with a Sumi brush and water
color abstraction.

"She has nowhere else to go. Her birthday is in two days, she'll be eleven." What the hell am I doing? The records said she set fires, stole, molested younger children, and punched your last foster mother. But I knew you were the one, you were the one; we needed to meet, to be yoked together at the heart. I needed to read to you at bedtime, braid your nappy hair, tell you about bleeding and tampons, leave sanitary pads in your bathroom, argue about make-up and halter tops, praise you at parent-teacher conferences (praise you to your face so you heard the words come from me, not second-hand, there was too much second-hand in your life already.)

I thought it would hurt more than it did when I called your caseworker to tell her I couldn't adopt you and they should probably find you another home before the holidays. Of course I cried, a throat-rattling cry. It took two years to find you, two years of forms and foster parent classes on Attachment Disorder and head lice. And prayers and candles lit to show you the way to me, and prayers and eight months of insemination because maybe, just maybe you were coming through my uterus, and then bleeding, and screaming, "What, God? What are you asking me to do?" and more prayers and then the phone call two days before your birthday.

I needed to hold your spindly body between my open knees, while you punched your bedroom wall and screamed, "I hate you, you fuckin' bitch. You're not my mother. I want my mother." I needed to know I could hold you through your rage and my fear. I needed to know I could hold you through this collision of love.

I needed to know
I could love you no matter
what you needed

Your rage! We both knew you could kill me. You locked yourself in the bathroom. I locked myself in my bedroom, called your caseworker at midnight to say I can't do this. But I needed to know, so I found the key. I found you, curled in the dry tub, clutching all the blankets you owned. Was this a porcelain protection for you, or for me? "Come back to bed," I whispered through my upset. I'll sing you a song. Finally, tears came. I didn't know you could cry. Of course I cried. You curled again between my legs, pressing your head against my breast, your mouth so close to my nipple. You apologized in pre-pubescent awkwardness, "Sorry I touched your boobie." I smelled the top of your head, "That's okay sweetie." You pressed closer as if trying to crawl back into the womb, the womb you could have come from, but didn't. You came from a poisoned womb that poisoned you and yet you still survived. I am your eighth foster mother in seven years.

Tomorrow we will
find mother number nine, but
tonight I need to
know if I can hold your hardened
body like the mother
I would want to be.

Ruby

Karen Campbell

Ruby, my beloved beauty school mannequin, waited indifferently, her faceless form impaled on my countertop standing by for her twelfth shampoo-set. I was startled out of my Zen pin curls. Unannounced, Ruby was my mother. My heart collapsed on itself. It is amazing how the body tucks away fifteen years of grief and unpacks instantly at the sound of music or the sight of a matronly hair-do.

I am not a pretty crier. I turn Scottish pink and blotchy, my chin bumps into cottage cheese under a torture-rack grimace. My nostrils flare and drip more than my eyes. Poor Haley Rose, my youngest, inherited the same embarrassment. Luckily the salon was buzzing. I tucked my tears into hair funnels and silver clips. Busyness is survival in prison.

The women's prison hair design program is an oasis in acres of concrete. Our leader speaks the language of ambition, creating a stir of optimism. Ten women inmates dressed in forest green scrubs serve up a little human touch and a few minutes of grace. It is all women, all estrogen, and it was my turn for tears.

I named the mannequin Ruby for her sass. Ruby gets a better table for dinner reservations. She wears clothes on the edge of 39. That day she was lurking in my booth working up her disguise as my mother. I know how this works. I saw the doll episode on "The Twilight Zone."

How could I have missed her before; the backcombing, the Dippity Do, the bubble cut? My childhood fluttered around me settling into three images of my mother's hair: riding in the car, getting ready for dinner out, and waking me for school.

In the 1960s and 70s the station wagon was the Campbell's conveyance of choice. My sister and I rode seatbelt-less in the back with the seats folded down. We set up Cleopatra's barge with Coleman sleeping bags and Winnie the Pooh characters lined up under the rear window. We drove as far as the freeway to spend the rest of the journey sick as dogs and rolling around like firewood.

My parents were oblivious to the rising bile of their silent passengers. My mother brought forth the quilted pink box of prickly rollers and silver clips and began setting her hair.

My father sang out, "Val de ree, val de rah...." splitting lyric fragments with humming and bubbly tuba solos. He would repeat the same stanza for about 50 miles with the same gaps in memory until "The Wanderer" became Pavlovian queasiness.

My mother perched cheerfully in the front seat using the glove compartment as a slicing board for cheddar cheese and Triscuits. In between jolly crunching she would insist we raise our green faces to see nature's wonderments: The Corn Palace, Bambi or one of Minnesota's 10,000 lakes. The further her hair was set, the more jaw action could be seen. Occasionally, to my horror, my mother's mouth would bark out a laugh or some other dramatics. Her cheesy Triscuit chunks loosed the restrained cataracts of vomit from both sisters all over the 100 Acre Wood. It is a wonder I eat cheese at all.

My mom was Jackie Kennedy. Her accoutrements included Chanel style suits and boxes of shoes with coordinating purses. The pill box hats nestled into sugar spun bouffants. I traipsed along after her with my trolls and Colorforms to the beauty parlor. She left looking cotton candy; I dragged my feet home in a childish pixie. It exposed my overbite and magnified my gangliness. I looked like a boy.

That evening, I sat on my mother's glamorous bed and helped her pack her matching purse while she dressed for dinner out. I have a picture of myself in that damn pixie, holding a black patent leather clutch, smiling unselfconsciously, adored by the queen. My mother is standing beside me dressed, her hair an impeccable Dear Abby. During this ritual, I was granted the privilege of winding the music key on her jewelry box and pawing through the plunder. I tried on a big girl personality with a pure heart, untainted by cynicism and doubt.

My hands continue to pin curl Ruby's crown. I ache for that innocence. I wish I could tell her just one more time how elegant she was.

I certainly passed on that chance as a snarling teen. I woke to Marge Simpson's forbear poking her cone into my bedroom urging food before school or some other such nonsense. Maybe if she ditched the state fair sleep cap, picked out the side and rebutressed the Notre Dame I could swallow a resentful thimble of orange juice. I was the poster child of L'Enfante Terrible. Forty years later, Mother Nature spanked my teenage angst with knees made of glass and crêpe neck skin. Ruby remains ageless.

Ruby carries herself as tastefully as she did twenty years ago. Twenty years from now, she will be a savvy Betty Crocker and that's the point. Our treasured elders are folding forward. They wear clodhoppers and carry Ben Gay in their shoulder purses but by God, their hair is perfect. It hasn't changed in 45 years. It is their identity and a fragile hold on a time when their daughters watched them apply lipstick with heroine worship.

Layers of my mother's memories are nudged into consciousness by hearing Julie Andrews sing Camelot or tasting our family's food group, cream of mushroom soup. When I am sick, I still want my mom to rub my back when I throw up. She is in my skin. I have her creases and smile. In the mirror behind Ruby's head I see my mother looking back at me.

I comb out Ruby's tangles more tenderly now. Perhaps by honoring her quiet, ladylike dignity, my mother's spirit will see the gawky child who still adores her mother.

The Jackhammer's Song

Richelle Morgan

It starts at 7 in the morning.

Jill wakes at 6:57, like always. She glances at the clock to confirm her internal punctuality, then turns to watch the sun dappling the leaves of the peach tree outside their bedroom window. She stretches her toes under the coverlet and allows herself to feel a spark of hope for the first time in months. Then the hammering begins.

"Jesus God!" Adam groans as he starts awake. "What is that? What time is it? Jill sits on the edge of the bed, her back to him as she pulls on her summer-weight robe. "Sounds like a jackhammer."

Adam flops his arms and legs heavily on the bed and sighs, "Nice way to wake up in the morning! Where are you going?"

"I'm going to make coffee," she says as she slips out the door.

"So," he says when he comes into the kitchen, shirtless and barefoot, a pair of shorts pulled over his boxers, "I guess you're still upset?"

She is standing with her hip leaning against the counter, her straight sandy hair falling in front of her face as she watches the coffee drip into the pot. The noise of the jackhammer is less here on the other side of the house, but she still has to speak loudly.

"Why should I be upset?" It feels good to have an excuse to shout.

Adam mutters to himself and stomps over to the cupboard where they keep the mugs. His legs are taut and muscled from a summer of running, but no matter how hard he works, the bulges on either side of his waist never completely disappear.

"Wait," she says.

"Wait what?"

"Wait until it's all brewed."

141

His eyes are flat as he takes out a mug and sets it next to the coffee pot. Without saying anything, he turns and walks out of the room. Jill hears the front door slam shut over the jackhammer, then a few moments later, the rustling of newspaper as the machine's engine dies.

She knows it is wearing on him, her moods, the sorrow that lies heavier on her shoulders each month. But she has no energy to coddle or reassure him, and she can't understand how he can ignore her struggle, their struggle.

When the coffee is done, she pours two mugs, and adds cream to his. She remembers the joy she used to take in making his coffee, creating the perfect balance of milk and bean, just for Adam. She wonders if he ever noticed.

The jackhammer re-starts as soon as she crosses the threshold into the living room, where Adam, his bare feet propped up on the coffee table, reads the sports page.

"I think it must be Bill," she shouts as she sets his coffee on a coaster and pulls out the Living section. "Dot mentioned getting rid of the patio and putting in brick."

Adam flips the newspaper over and continues reading.

Before Jill has a chance to turn to the advice column she always reads first, Adam flings his section of the paper aside with a sigh. "We might as well get something done, since relaxing is impossible," he says.

Jill puts down her paper and climbs the stairs to their bedroom. As she dresses, Adam makes a list, neatly drawing check-off boxes next to each task.

By noon, Adam is prowling around the house with a hammer, a pencil and picture hooks, hanging all the prints and framed photos they've been meaning to get to. Jill has just figured out the self-cleaning feature on the oven, and she is taking her bucket of bleach water to the refrigerator shelves.

Jill's nostrils burn as she listens to Adam's frantic hammering, just barely audible over the jackhammer. Every time the machine stops, she can feel her neck muscles start to relax, only to have them seize up again as soon as it roars back to life.

"I've got to get out of here," Adam shouts behind her during a sustained burst.

She looks at him over her shoulder. "Lunch?" she says, miming eating a sandwich.

They are silent in the car, speak only when necessary at the pub. On the drive home, she takes a deep breath and tries again.

"It's really no big deal," she says. "You just go in the office with me and do your thing, they do their thing and that's it. Dr. Sanger said that in a case like ours, there's a good chance it will work on the first try."

Adam flips through two of their pre-programmed radio stations before turning it off altogether.

"If this doesn't work, I promise, I promise I'll let it go."

"I haven't changed my mind." He speaks gently, but there is something underneath it, a finality she has been ignoring for months, that irritates her.

"So that's just it? You've decided and I should—what?"

"It's not a matter of deciding, Jill. It just is the way it is. I've accepted it, and you should too. All this…" he waves his hand in the air, searching for a word, then gives up and continues, "isn't good for you, for us."

"What about last night? You said there were options! This is an option!"

"Not for me."

She realizes then what he had really been saying last night, understands that he was trying to gently inure her to the idea. But hearing it now, just as they drive past the park where she used to walk in the evenings, where the sight of children playing had once fueled her dreams, she feels as if she has been slapped.

Adam turns the car onto their street, pulls into the driveway. He turns off the car and keeps his eyes on his hands, resting, as always, at ten and two on the steering wheel.

The jackhammer is running in short bursts, chipping away at Jill's composure as Adam turns to her and says, "I'm sorry, but we need to move on, look to the future. It just wasn't meant to be."

He smiles the sad half-smile that has replaced the sly, gap-toothed grin she used to love so well and goes into the house. Jill sits in the car until the heat makes breathing too difficult, then joins Adam inside to continue checking chores off the list.

They sit together on the porch steps, late-day sun glinting off the ice in their droplet-covered glasses of lemonade. She sees him open his mouth to say something, to appease her perhaps, but it is useless. The noise of the jackhammer splits the warm afternoon into fragments.

She remembers a day two years ago when they sat on the porch steps one evening in late spring, only they were drinking iced tea then. They had just found out she was expecting a baby, and they couldn't stop smiling, even as they talked about how frightened they were. Adam had such plans for fixing up the spare bedroom as a nursery, and Jill, though tired, was anxious to get the rest of the boxes unpacked from their move two weeks before.

In her memory, it is two different people entirely sitting on this porch. That couple, young and filled with equal parts hope and fear, went on to have a baby, a boy. He is just over a year now, toddling around on fat little legs while his parents chase after him and try to keep him from eating the houseplants.

That couple is probably thinking about the day when they'll have another, hopefully a girl. Maybe they, too, are sitting on the porch this evening, drinking lemonade and laughing as their son pulls at the grass and flings it in the air, babbling in a half-language that only they understand.

That couple won't ever know the terms "incompetent cervix" or "unex-plained secondary infertility" or that before 20 weeks it's a miscarriage and after, it's a stillbirth.

Adam had refused to hold the baby, but Jill, encouraged by the nurse and the social worker, took the tiny bundle in her arms. He was tiny, so tiny and so still. At 22 weeks, he weighed less than a pound, and there was nothing anyone could do.

She had felt guilty, of course. So had Adam, even though it was her body that had failed them. The doctor had assured her that there were things that could be done, once she and Adam decided they were ready to try again.

So they grieved for a season, then started over. She began buying her pregnancy tests by the dozen at the dollar store. Adam stopped asking the results. It has been a blur, this past two years, of mysterious twinges and hope-filled pains, and Jill can't believe they have wasted so much time for so little gain.

Jill hadn't told him about yesterday's appointment with Dr. Sanger beforehand. She'd wanted to arm herself with Dr. Sanger's statistics and brochures, knowing her desire was not enough to convince him to go ahead with a risky and expensive procedure.

She approached him after she finished the dinner dishes. He sat on the sofa, his feet propped on the coffee table, his finger poised over the mute button on the remote control. Jill struggled to keep her voice from shaking as she told him about the appointment.

He sighed, then deflected all her statistics without once raising his voice. He balked at the money that, if spent, would decimate their retirement accounts. He repeated his wish that "no extreme measures" be taken. He wrapped his long-fingered hand around hers and said, "Honey, let's just try to examine all of our options."

But Jill could sense his anger and disappointment. She knew he hated her tendency to hold a problem close, to worry at it until its significance outstripped Adam's ability to deal with it. He was so logical, so efficient, so self-sufficient. If his prescribed course of action turned out to be fruitless, then so be it. He could walk away and never look back. But she never thought he could be that way about having a child. If you wanted a child, you did what you had to do until you had one. That fact was so simple in Jill's mind that she felt Adam's intransigence must simply be fear. She felt certain that she could ease his anxieties, if only she could find the right combination of logic and facts and orderly steps to take. His rejection of her carefully collected data was crushing.

But she held onto his talk of "options" as she left him sitting in the lamp-lit room, skipping across television channels without pausing to see what was on.

But this afternoon, the sun hot on her hair, she understands that there aren't as many options anymore. She knows they can't go back to that other life they once lived, one filled with lazy mornings spent in her tiny bed with rumpled blue and pink flowered sheets. Surrounded by the clutter that adorned her small studio apartment, they had talked and talked, legs entwined, hands tracing each other's faces, still learning every plane and curve, but she could not recall, now, anything they had said.

She tells herself again that he is simply tired, that the strain of hope, dashed each month, is getting to him. She thinks that if she could give him this one thing, it might, if not erase, then certainly blur, the grief they have been carrying between them.

She watches him tapping his toes in his sandals and hears his voice say "no extreme measures" in her head. It occurs to her that she may have been grieving alone all this time.

The jackhammer stops its assault on the concrete, and Jill and Adam both let out the breath they have not realized they are holding.

"Maybe he's finished," Adam says, clinking the ice in his glass.

Jill is surprised at how pleasing the sound is, how the ringing glass soothes her after the fits and starts of the jackhammer.

"There've been pauses before," she says. A tiny black ant crawls around her sandal, then disappears over the edge of the stoop. The moment, this moment, surprises her with its near-perfection. The late summer sun brings pleasant pricks of sweat to her neck, and the soft smell of lavender drifts by on the breeze. But there's the smell of concrete dust, too, and Adam's pastrami breath. And there are all the ants. Maybe that's what perfect is, she thinks, having the bad next to the good and still finding pleasure.

But then Adam clears his throat, and the moment slides away like one of the beads of water on her glass.

"So. Are we going to be OK?" he asks.

In the jackhammer's silence, Jill reacquaints herself with the sounds of her neighborhood—a bird, the small ones that sing so much this time of year, is warbling in a nearby tree. There's the buzz of traffic from the main street a few blocks over, and a strange summer hum lying just beneath the surface of it all. She can hear, too, the neighbor children playing basketball at the end of the street. She doesn't even feel the hard place in her chest anymore when she hears them laugh, but she knows it's there.

"I don't know, Adam," she says, and in using his name, remembers the joy she used to take in saying it and hearing it said.

She remembers telling him she wanted to name their first son Adam, and his saying the baby should have his own name. So they had settled on David Adam. Girls' names were so much harder—Adam liked plain, no-nonsense names like Sarah and Jane, while Jill preferred grander-sounding names like Annabelle and Josephine. Elizabeth, she thinks. I bet we could have agreed on that, and it stuns her that she never thought of it until now.

"I don't know," she says again, but she is lying.

She doesn't know when it changed. After the baby, they had seemed even closer, had sensed each other's thoughts and feelings, faced their despair together, united. But of course, that was when they thought they could just, after a period of mourning, have another.

Adam is staring into his glass, watching the ice swirl around, waiting for her to tell him their future. His dark hair, the thick, wavy mane she has long envied, is falling forward, and she fights the old urge to push it back.

Once more, the jackhammer soars across the notes of its song with aggressive abandon, a long burst, followed by two short, long, long, short, long. Jill grits her teeth, and her fingers tighten on her glass. The noise goes on so long that she begins to believe it will never cease, that the deafening rattle will be forever ringing in her ears. A cloud of dust rises beyond the fence next door.

And then it stops.

Over the ringing in her ears, she hears Bill call out, "Crack open a beer, Dot! I'm done!"

Adam laughs and says, "Thank God." He raises his glass to Jill, forgetting, it seems, that he's been waiting for her at all.

Jill stands up and dusts off the seat of her shorts. She looks down at Adam, and she thinks she can see a tiny sliver of sadness in his eyes before he turns away.

"Do you remember," he says as he stares at his feet, "that little apartment on Market Street? How we used to lounge around, talking and laughing for hours?" He sniffs a dry laugh. "They call it dating, but I don't recall us going out very much."

"Yes," she says, surprised to hear that he ever looks back.

"What did we even talk about all those times?"

"I don't remember."

He looks up at her again, the sadness more evident this time. "Me neither."

Again she thinks of that tiny bed, pushed under the one window in her studio apartment. From that vantage, they could see the street so clearly. They had known exactly what was coming, and it was so easy to imagine where things were going. In the whirlwind of marriage, moving, pregnancy and loss, she had forgotten how comfortable that cramped and cluttered apartment had been.

She looks at their house, sees the peach tree that stands guard outside their bedroom window, and wonders how she could ever have considered this home.

They are on the front porch again, only it is morning. Adam is hunched into a sweatshirt and shorts, his bare toes curled over the edge of the top step. Jill stands next to him, turned only slightly toward him, and rocks from foot to foot in her favorite pair of sandals.

Across the street, Bill is standing in the bed of a pert little blue pick-up, hoisting in the jackhammer as his wife stands in the driveway fussing.

"It's only for a little while," Jill tells Adam again.

"Yeah," he says.

It feels good to call his bluff. Jill is giddy with her own bravery, and she toys with the idle notion that in a few months' time, she could already have met someone new, the future father of the baby she knows she is meant to have. There is nothing Adam can do now but change his mind or lose her forever. She thinks this is the most powerful she has ever felt.

Adam looks up and moves to hug her goodbye. And in that instant before his arms come around her, she sees the merest hint of moistness in his familiar brown eyes. Her triumph melts into terror, and she grips him tighter than she wants to. He pulls away before she is ready to let him go.

"I guess we'll talk when you're ready. Settled, I mean," Adam says as he watches Bill strap down the jackhammer.

Jill follows his gaze. Dot hovers around the truck, offering suggestions on the best way to use the bungee cords. Bill grunts in response, but Jill can see that he is following his wife's instructions to the letter. When the jackhammer is secured, Bill hops down, kisses his wife, and drives away. As the truck pulls out of the driveway, Jill sees the mounded pile of rubble that used to be their neighbor's patio, and she fights an urgent need to weep.

Instead, she takes a deep breath and picks up her overnight bag, settling the strap on her shoulder. Jill tosses a weak smile at Adam as she lifts her foot and steps off the porch.

Quantum

Sage Cohen

Nothing is less real than realism....
Details are confusing. It is only by selection, by elimination,
by emphasis, that we get at the real meaning of things.

— GEORGIA O'KEEFFE

From all possibilities: this
coat keeping warm from throat
to moment. Strung like street
from yellow line to yellow line.
The red-hatted lady sloshes by.
Not quite cohesive enough for story,
the notes hover like photographs.
Each one shouldering the weight
of articulation. My car shudders
with not enough. My eye sockets
dark as a harbor relearning
the art of return after war
stripped the world of metal and fear.
I should have given you a reason
to stay. I didn't see how
the trees could divide. I could give
you green. I could feed you fiction.
The waitress asks me, "Just one?"
as if I were not enough. And yet
the room can barely contain me.
There is no justice. And no waitress
to serve its unanswerable demands.

Eggs and Butter and Faith

Sage Cohen

the dogs have followed me
downstairs like heartbreak.
sadness is our habit.
i cannot find kindness
on the shelves.
i have no recipe.
only eggs and butter and faith.
there is no saving
grace, no blame,
no place of rest.
until i trust the sun
to its own descent,
forgiveness breaks me
down to dust the waves
carry me out over
the years i listened
to you leaving me,
the sound of it trapped
in my ocean ear
as the conch curls
her tidal heart
against the thin
shimmering of moon's
slivered grief.

I Make You a River

Sage Cohen

Philip Levine claims that there was at least one day when Lorca and Crane were in the same place at the same time. His poem is the imagined moment of flint on flint, as the poets' minds converged in a small brush fire of tongue and ash before each fell forward into his own, inevitable future.

Stranded in my own moment in time, the electric pulse of poetry charging my clinging sweater, back lined up with the hard bench of listening, I enter the eternity of Spring, where Lorca stands stooped, his pockets weighted with unspent poems.

Each hard knuckle of bud containing a great courage of reckless beauty unfurls into words under the spell of my recording pen.

Levine says: "horse cock and mattress stuffing," the name for a sandwich composed of Wonder bread and bologna. We can take any experience and make it matter: put it in a barn or on a train, or blast it with headlights. I make you a river, so my love has somewhere to go.

I take the word "sacred" into me, and assign it to your mouth, which is echoing my inner ear as the conch holds the ocean. We are blind as a field. I am a maple tree wide as century, your kiss the sun pouring through my green. Time rings me in radiance. There is only this moment of enough. Stable as seed, your hands hold all futures. My pollens drift to dust.

The little note cards on my knee are preserved petals. Levine claims he hasn't met a poet who rivals Dickenson. We silence our beauty inside the heavy book of Past. These cascading evasions we call time and truth, around which we organize our disappearances, return me to the cross-hatched convergence of afternoon and future. The earth's thirst for metaphor rains you over my listening skin. I breathe you in, then cry you out again. I write you down so when the river returns, it will know to flow right through me.

Elsewhere

the same sky for us all

Elsewhere

Paulann Petersen

Returned from night, the sky
looks back at our city with newly
blue eyes. What it saw on the other side
of this world while most of us slept
would have kept us from sleep
had we been looking too. Enemy rockets
blew up the approximate spot
from which rockets had screeched toward them
the day before. Tit for tat, on and on, there,
in their daytime while most of us slept.
A notch in the aimer's weapon. A crater
in the target's terrain. Cities, villages erupt
with ulcers of crumbled concrete,
broken stone. We watch on TV.

The only sound here is tire on asphalt
a block away, a breeze through the top
of this neighborhood's tallest trees.
The only rubble is blossoms fallen
in a moist heap under the hibiscus.
Those few pollen-laden bees
too old, too tattered to fly away
are the only casualties in sight. Left from night
is what the sky saw below itself
while we slept. The heavens that covered—
just hours ago—another half of the world with blue.
The same sky for us all.

Storybook

Paulann Petersen

She'd lifted her face right off the pages of a book we'd read in Miss Bertha Harrison's third grade room. She had a pencil-line face to match her strings of arms and legs sticking out from a cotton wash dress' faded plaid. She was a live girl who matched a book-girl in a story about bowls of dust. The Dust-Bowl. Story of crops gone so gray that a whole family loaded its blankets and clock and crib onto a truck and moved west across the westward turning pages of a picture book in our Portland, Oregon schoolroom.

She had the exact face of that story-girl looking like a shrunken version of her gray-eyed, brow-puckered story-mother walking in a world of washed-out colors. They walked along thin dirt roads where dust rose in puffs made from a pencil's lead laid flat and brushed along paper.

She was alive in our room at Richmond School, the new girl so much unlike our Dick and Jane, bright red ball, green grass, Look! See! lives, that she might have come from a whole other corner of the world, except she didn't. Yet did, because I was sure I'd seen her first on the pages of that Dust-Bowl book.

Thin in a way that I—thin as I was—would never be, quiet in a way my wisps of shyness could scarcely understand, she came and she went for weeks. And then didn't. Baby sister, a newborn, Miss Harrison said, and this new girl's absence for the past week was something we could maybe understand. Some family strangeness had wrapped around her house so tightly she couldn't put on that one plaid wash dress she wore, slip the strands of her brown hair into their braids, slip herself out the door and off to school in those days after her baby sister arrived.

Show and Tell were words we waited for each week, a chance to bring a birthday toy (once my doll Elizabeth Ann who walked on feet big enough to need a real baby's shoes), or something strange like the box of baby pigs my mother borrowed from a fellow nurse who knew a farmer. Piglet! Piglet! we cried, as we each got a turn holding a tiny mass of twisting soft-skinned pink over the box in case we faltered and dropped that squealing baby.

At home, said the new girl now back at school, My sister was born at home, and I could bring to mind only those pink faces above their cones of wrapped blanket at the hospital where my mother worked. Born at our house, she said. Her turn to tell for Show and Tell, and some separate world holding her was spinning slowly away from the known world where my feet rested. I delivered Mama's baby myself, at home. Then silence. Then Miss Harrison's fumbled stop to Show and Tell, the Everybody back to your desks, go on, hurry now. Her hand on the new girl's jut of shoulder, nudging her along. Let's open our books to today's story, while color rose in my babied face, but not a bit of red showed in the dustbowl face of that storybook girl, new in our class at school.

The Pantanal

Katherina Audley

I wanted to visit the Pantanal. One hundred and forty thousand square miles of mushy savannah speckled with jaguars and crawling with crocodiles sounded great to me. Anacondas slithering all over the place. This was a place to see, but not without a machete-wielding local by my side. Individual guides charged a hefty fee, so I forced my groupaphobia into the recesses of my mind and booked a budget tour through the hostel where I was staying on the border of Brazil and Paraguay.

I left the next day. At the crack of dawn, to be more specific. A gaggle of Brazilian girls was hanging out in the bus terminal parking lot. They were all ready for a fun, sexy day in their meticulous eyeliner, fleshy muffin tops brimming out over skintight jeans, and precarious heels. They didn't appear to be going anywhere. I felt awkward and apart. Notably unsexy. My hair was carelessly shoved under a bandana. The best thing that could be said about my light blue shirt was that it didn't have any major stains on it. I reflexively reached for my lip gloss, a lightweight concession to my vanity.

The best estimate I could get on how far we were from the Pantanal was six hours. Too long a time to share a bus seat if I could help it. As the last of the double seats filled up, new boarders slowed down and attempted eye contact. I knew the routine. Their pause was my cue to look up, make eye contact, nod and smile warmly, meaning, "Yes. You are welcome to be my seatmate." Instead, I played dirty, covering the seat next to me with clothes and books, blew my nose a few times and scattered the tissues around for good measure. Loud, snotting colds are highly effective seat-mate repellent.

I had scanned the sign-up sheet when I joined this tour, and knew that the tour group was composed of a baker's dozen of young Israelis, a young couple from France, a 45-year-old Canadian architect and a 37-year-old British male, whose profession, tantalizingly, was listed as "Sound Recordist." I pictured a tall, pale, bespectacled type earnestly holding his fuzzy mike way up high to capture sounds of exotic birds and insects singing in the trees. I had always wanted to record the twitters, calls and occasional shrieks of the jungle. I looked forward to meeting him, once we were in the Pantanal and he already had his mike set up and I had gotten some sleep.

The Sound Recordist boarded the bus. He was not tall or bespectacled. He was pale, though. He paused by my seat to see if I would do the right thing—make eye contact, smile, nod. I refused his gaze. He passed to the back of the bus looking for an open seat. He came back to my snot-covered book-infested empty seat, and told me that it was the only seat left on the bus. I moved my stuff over. The Sound Recordist sat down.

The gringo trail in South America is glutted with recent college graduates from Europe and Israelis, aged 21 to 24, fresh out of the army, most of whom are just finding out what it is like to be on the road for the first time. Although the Sound Recordist had left his sound equipment at home, he was rich in travel stories which were shared with a humbleness and gratitude for having had such opportunities which kept our story swapping from becoming a spitting match. His name was Glenn.

There was one other non-South American person on the bus. He was of the 21-24 year old fresh out of the Israeli army demographic. I could tell this by his hair. After two mandatory years of Israeli army high and tights, he was making up for lost hair expression time with a giant black, curly cloud that I estimated to be eight months long. An exceedingly artistic goatee and mustache added to the overall effect. A pair of wire framed glasses made him seem more bohemian than hippy. We dubbed him The Mad Professor.

After bouncing along for five hours, the bus dropped Glenn, The Mad Professor and me off on the porch of a rickety tin shack, standing alone in the middle of the open savannah.

An old man wearing obscenely threadbare jean shorts and ancient flip flops hobbled out from inside and let us in to what turned out to be a store. The unspoken agreement was that the price to occupy his porch for an undetermined period of time was the purchase of some dusty goodies. We poked through his wares and selected fake Hawaiian Punch and chocolate. He closed the store again and disappeared inside. It rained. A flock of parakeets passed by. Three dogs sized like nesting dolls came by and engaged in a threesome on the porch. We drank our punch and watched.

The Mad Professor was full of dread about the notoriously ravenous Pantanal mosquitoes. He believed that mosquitoes found him especially delicious. Every time he saw a mosquito, he preemptively attacked it, marking his kill with a triumphant cry. Glenn shared that he was lucky to be exceptionally hairy, as his thick chest, arm, leg and back fur created an impenetrable barricade against hungry proboscises. I wished I still smoked because cigarettes deterred mosquitoes and made buses appear. We had been sitting there for 8 hours. Our punch was gone. So were the chocolates. The charm of the Mad Professor's battle cries, Glenn's body hair and the nesting dogs had worn thin long ago.

Our truck appeared just after dark. I did not want to clamber into the back of that pickup truck with a dozen other stinky, muddy backpackers. Fortunately my chick status landed me bitch seat in the cab, which was a mixed blessing. The driver stank worse than the backpackers and the guy riding shotgun was a groper. As a result, I spent a few bumpy hours negotiating fingers. The groper would put one finger on, say, my outer thigh, and if I let him keep it there for longer than a certain period of time, he would try two fingers, which sometimes was okay, but a palm was not, so he would get a shove in the ribs. Then the truck would jolt and we would bump around and his hand would land on, say, my arm, which allowed one or two fingers, but again, no thumbs, no palm. Eventually, my outer thigh became a kind of no man's land where he was permitted to rest one fingertip, but that was it. I was tired of it, but when I turned around to see Glenn and company banging around on top of twelve giant backpacks in the back of the pickup truck, which was trundling through eighteen inches of mud in the rain in the dark, I continued my nonverbal negotiations with the groper.

The groper had offered to be my guide since we were getting along so well. I hurt his feelings by expressing a preference for another guide who some returning tourists at the hostel had recommended.

That particular guide was taking the week off, it turned out. The sulking groper got assigned to the Israeli gang because he spoke some Hebrew. Glenn and I got assigned to the Colonel along with the French couple and the Canadian architect. The Colonel called Glenn, Claire, for some reason, so we started calling him Betty, but I don't think he noticed. Anyway, Colonel Betty hated Israelis with a vitriol I had previously associated with radical terrorist nuts, and was openly scornful of most other gringos, as well. He found our mosquito bite tolerance wimpy, our flip flops noisy and our broken Portuguese pathetic and told us so with condescending snorts and glares if we so much as swatted a bug, walked a step or said a word.

The camp was like something out of Survivor but without the gimmicks, styling or subtly placed merchandising. We were shuffled into a big octagonal screened-in palapa with 20+ hammocks arranged like spokes around a central pole. Glenn's bad back couldn't survive sleeping in a hammock and my groupaphobia skyrocketed to emergency levels. We finagled our way into the guides' more spacious palapa and managed to land two tents of our own. The Israeli army graduates were having a sing-a-long as they settled in. My scummy tent on the hard ground suddenly seemed like the Ritz Carlton.

Early the next morning we were marchmarchmarched out of bed and into the jungle to see some wildlife, goddammit. Colonel Betty scornfully led us through this thicket and that complaining about our loud flip flops, our stinky insect repellent and our general gringo ineptitude, which was surely the thing that was keeping all the wildlife away. We saw some monkeys, storks, weird little mammals and a few parakeets before Betty got fed up and commanded us back to eat and rest before the afternoon march.

My dehydration and exhaustion transformed into a full scale migraine with all the bells and whistles, during our siesta. While the others were being marched through the swamps, I lay in my hammock popping painkillers, throwing them back up again, and explaining to cowboy after cowboy who came in to check me out, offer me tea, coffee, massage, water, aspirin and so on that I would be okay. I kept opening my eyes to find big eyes searching my face in the dusky light, strong rough hands stroking my forehead, howler monkeys were moaning and howling and I just wished I weren't so sick. I awoke fully recovered before daybreak, just in time for a fishing trip. 0430 found us all in the back of the truck (well, not me, I was riding bitch again with a sulky groper) en route to a murky swamp full of alligators to fish for piranhas.

We hooked steak onto our hooks and waded into the water, which felt like about the dumbest, most counterintuitive thing one could possibly do. I think they took us there before we were fully awake because otherwise there was no way we could be cajoled into wading into sludgy water with our meat hooks as alligators slithered by. It only took a short time to acclimate to the alligators' presence as the meat was continuously being tugged off of our hooks by hungry piranhas and within a few hours everyone had caught something. We were all quite pleased with ourselves for being such good hunter/gatherers and proudly took pictures of our pile of dead piranhas stacked on a board next to a rusty machete stuck into the ground with some alligators lingering in the background, hoping for scraps. But then the truck driver reappeared from the other side of the swamp with as many fish hanging off his single string as 16 of us had collectively caught in the same period of time.

This was an industrial strength budget backpacker's Pantanal tour. The food was continuously recycled from one meal to the next, the mosquito nets were holey, and the guides were not the kind of animal aficionados you'd expect in a place where you literally bump into tapirs and capybaras on your way to pee. They feigned a thinly veiled enthusiasm about the wildlife that suggested they would have been shooting these stupid animals if us bleeding hearts weren't around taking all of the fun out of it. Nonetheless, I was warming up to these rough and loose Pantanal cowboys who lived like a bunch of overgrown Lost Boys from Peter Pan. They never got tired of playing lasso the cow skull or scare the gringo with live tarantulas and snakes. They played the same Brazilian Cowboy songs over and over again dancing with a women if there was a willing one nearby and with each other if not. They threw back great swigs of cheap, fiery *cachaca* out of the bottle, and swapped hats, shorts, shirts, towels and girls indiscriminately. Every week the slate was washed clean as one group of tourists ebbed out and a new one flowed in. Every so often, a girl would stick. After being fed tender, choice morsels of piranha or wild boar meat and adorned with hand-woven crocodile tooth and palm frond jewelry by a cowboy or two, she would select the one she wanted and retire with him to his tent for a few days or weeks. The newer girls still joined in on horse rides and fishing trips with tourists. Girls who had been around longer invariably had succumbed to an impulse to clean things up around camp with frustrating results. The cowboys were happy to share out their new acquisitions' belongings with the rest of the camp. Nice, clean girl towels, hotel soap, Aveda shampoo and toothpaste were enthusiastically used up. The girls harbored resentments about these things. Although they were free to catch a ride out at any time, they seemed to be straining against an invisible net to break free of the place.

Our guides pulled on jeans for the afternoon and hopped barefoot onto their horses. The Israeli army graduates, led by the Mad Professor, loudly

161

hiya'd their horses into frantic gallops, much to the guides' chagrin. Glenn and the Canadian used the reins on their horses like brakes on a runaway train, even though their saggy backed horses would have been turned into glue long ago if they had lived anywhere other than the Pantanal. My horse was the kind of horse that was the happiest with its nose lodged in the butt of the horse in front of it, so we cruised along that way most of the time. When my horse got near the French girl's horse, she said in her salty French girl way, "My horse does not like your horse" and so I did my best to keep my horse's nose up a different horse's butt. It didn't show much of a preference. We chased big white brahma bulls around the fields and scared cranes into flight until sunset.

The groper was with us, riding like a maniac. He was such a tiny dirty little thing who was lost in his riding leathers and too big hat but there was one moment during sunset when he pulled off his hat when no one was looking except for me and his hair fell rippling black and curly all the way down his back and his horse was doing exactly what he wanted it to. Backlit by the setting sun, he was breathtakingly gorgeous for just one moment. But then he saw me looking at him in wonder and trotted over, smirking, with his groping hand tentatively outstretched. The negotiations were fired up again.

After dark, a warm, soft rain fell and the generator blinked out. I abandoned the beer I was nursing at the makeshift bar and landed in a hammock with one of the cowboys getting a just-a-foot-then-a-hand-then-an-everything massage. All twelve guides had offered me such services at some point, and in the darkness I couldn't tell which one I was with. Lightning flashed. In that flash of electric blue brightness, a piercing in his chin caught the light. I made a mental note to ID him using that facial decoration in the morning. As clothes came off, his style became more bitey and slappy than I preferred. His bedroom talk was limited to, "Oh please. I have condom. Please. Sex? Yes? I have condom. Yes?" The combination of sudden, firm whacks to my unsuspecting rear coupled with his repetitive, limited bedroom lexicon nipped my passion in the bud. The generator roared back into action and I feigned hunger, ending my fumble in the jungle with a cowboy whose name I never quite caught.

Every previous sexual encounter of mine had been painstakingly built up to: We met. We talked. Maybe we danced a bit. We parted ways. Several rounds of flirtatious telephone conversations and confessionary e-mails ensued, followed by hot drinks, expensive meals, alcohol, then, finally, bed. I was giddy and flabbergasted by this new system. We hadn't even properly introduced ourselves before going to bed!

Glenn blamed it on Brazil. He had spent months in this country, and assured me that it happens to everyone—Brazilians and non-Brazilians alike. Casual sex in Brazil is as common as going for a coffee with a new acquaintance is in the rest of the world.

Everything about Brazil inspires sex—the music, the language, the dancing, the scenery, the weather, the clothes, the food, but most of all the people because they are all thinking about screwing each other all the time and doing it as much as thinking about it. There are entire stores devoted to naughty Catholic schoolgirl minis and even fat old ladies rock spandex and let their bellies and bums squirt out between bulging seams because hey, it's flesh, wonderful flesh, this is big bum country after all and what is a bum for if not to jiggle and what is a belly for if not to hang on to. Brazilians come samba dancing out of their mama's wombs ready to out-fun the funnest of us and still have energy left over for making whoopy. I mean, honestly, let's see you samba dance for eight hours and still be shaking it, and it has nothing to do with being fit and everything to do with being fun.

The next morning, it was time to go. The groper, the pierced cowboy and Colonel Betty invited me to stay for another week, on the house. But a DJ friend of mine had taught me to always leave the nightclub in the middle of a great song, so my final memory of the night would be a fond one. My pierced no-name cowboy made me a necklace out of braided plant fiber and alligator teeth and just before I climbed into the truck to leave, he tugged me into his cabana for one last passionate kiss, punctuated by a little spank and tied it around my neck. I left the Pantanal aglow, with a great taste in my mouth.

Shoreline

Elizabeth Jones

I'm telling the story of sand
with my fingers tight around it.
These are bones, grains
of old creatures, of new creatures,
people I've never met.

Their eyes are the water
washing over me,
tumbling stone into sand
crushing bones into sand
seeing colors my eyes don't see
sifting shapes my hands can't hold.

The women of the village circle the well,
their hands on large jugs—
some clay, many plastic.
They talk of rain, new births,
children lost to war.
The sand blows dry around them.

Across the Way

Virginia Davis

across the way
a line of trees
bare branched in winter
and punctuated by low shrubs
state themselves
their slight and constant
variations of meaning
brought on by an east wind

A Morning Poem for Anne

My body is an old wheelbarrow
standing in place
at the foot of the garden.
Weathered wood,
rusted steel.
It is what it is.

Salt

Jenette Purcell

He hurries to cross the space between
To wash my silence with hope
As if love wasn't measured
By distance

By a tangle of unspoken words
Waiting like seaweed on the shore
Missed glances in the darkness
A certain way of sitting still
When love thrashes inside

Years were formed in moments
And it takes more than a breath now
To blow away the heaviness
More than the ocean
To stop the salt of tears

Back at the Station

Shanna Germain

Four years gone, the station sounds the same:
rigs rumble to warm, hoses wrap themselves tight
around reels, men slip into third-day turnouts,
while gray smoke rises up old flames. I gave

six years to hard lines and hatchets and boys who
trapped me in cars so they could break me free.
Six years of loving two smoke eaters at once,
tugging Doug's spent cigar scent from his tongue,

his red hair steaming wet wood, while Jimmy laid
hose on the barn burn five miles on.
I want those days back, nights too, when flames brought
everything to light. Even in the darkness

of the station, the rigs still shine red. My fingers
work the smooth skin of the pumper door, tug
seven gold letters spelling a company
I no longer keep. Turning, in the long
mirror, this face, dull and flat as a burnt-out
house. The siren sounds overhead, alarm
rising to realize its one true note: everywhere
but here, something stops to burn.

The Burrow

Allegra Heidelinde

She sat across the path, hand on her belly, and watched. Nothing stirred. Her feet got cold, her nose started to run. She tried not to sniff, but finally had to. She adjusted her position into a fetal crouch, lifting her damp bottom off the ground and crossing her arms over her knees. Her eyes never left the dark hole. She imagined it was warm inside, that it was deep enough to line with dry grasses and bits of fur—that it was close and warm and snug. She remembered childhood books, Benjamin Bunny, Winnie the Pooh and other small woodland creatures. Dressed in clothes and cuddled up with loved ones, tea and a pot of honey.

She so rarely tripped. Sure-footed and self-confident, "Half Billy goat!" her family used to tease. Today though, nothing felt right. The wet snow changed the landscape, her mood, loosened familiar rocks on the path. She tumbled, hands casting out, landing hard on the muddy trail. She'd seen the burrow, dark against the bright snow, as she fell.

Her knees began to hurt. She shifted again and wiped her nose on her sleeve. There was nothing more to do. Only the waiting. She listened to the melting snow drip. Listened to her breathing. Listened to the dim thud of her heart. Ba-dum. Ba-dum. Ba-dum.

It was all a mistake really. From start to finish, one big mistake. Snow slid off with a splatter and a fern sprang up, partially obscuring the open mouth of the burrow. She exhaled. At first it was all sweetness and promise, shyness and newness and hope.

When she knew and she was certain, she allowed herself the small joy of pretending it could be hers. "For just tonight," she promised herself, "For just tonight, it's yours." She'd slept with a smile on her face.

It was still too cold for comfort. The snow sent a steady chill up from the ground; her breath came out white moist clouds. Still, not one wet nose, not one whisker, not even a hint of a rustle from the burrow. It was dark, quiet and possibly abandoned. There were no tracks in the snow around it.

Nothing to indicate the last time it had been called home. She admired the graceful curve of the fern that arched over the opening. By tomorrow, I'd walk right past and never know it was here, she thought. The shadows were longer when she left her self-appointed post and picked her way down the cold mucky trail that had appeared so promising at the start.

Listen

Jane Galin

Why not just stop and listen beyond
as if to a river
or rain
or wind
or the sea;
by day and by night this going speaks to you
in a low voice.

I heard it
through the jumble of all my things,
what I piled against the door at night
and no one could climb over—
yet each noise
held my sleep at gunpoint.

I heard,
what happens if you notice
fear deep inside your body?
There it is,
and there it is
and it was always there.
But before that awful always
was this unlocatable
sound of wind,
sound of fire.

Just listen now, I heard.
Later you'll sleep
all the missing years of sleep,
including nightmares,
as you consent to meet, then part with fear;
and you may cry at losing something,
even the bullet
surgeons twist out of your heart
to save your life.

Cry, cry back
all the missing years of breath,
and then breathe soft.

Nothing owns you.
As if the gun could give its metal
back to the earth
where it never did harm,
for when you awaken
the dream belongs to you, not you to it—
you're free.

lightfastness, matins

Gwendolyn Morgan

Hemlock
heavy rain
chinook wind.
She ties

the threads
of light
in
coniferous wood
sap suffused with amber resin

shadows resist—
it is too early for delicacy
web of wood spider
bracken fern, trillium
wing of great horned owl

leap of brook trout.
She waits

prays the rosary of constellations
listens for red fox

to tell her
it is morning.

EXCERPT FROM

Other Than Words

Cynthia Richardson

PART ONE—SOPHIE

After Thomas died, I had everything to lose by not speaking. But muteness sets up house and relegates you to tenant status, exacting devotion and servitude because you have nowhere else to live: it is your body, your life. Sometimes survival requires striking a bargain.

His body was retrieved from Ring Lake not far from where we lived, the chapel-house, so named because it was originally a chapel in the northern Michigan woods. Thomas' mother and my family—parents, two brothers, a sister—arrived from the East coast to mourn, provide my daughter and myself with rudimentary care, and to try to make sense of it all. They wanted to think I had temporarily lost my mind from the shock, but more likely they were closer to believing that I decided to simply stop communicating. I was, after all, a dancer and choreographer, given to strange fits of introspection and moments of theatrics. It didn't occur to them there might be things I could not say aloud. Not yet; maybe never.

Janice, my younger sister, paced back and forth, her muddy shoes leaving dark stains on the wooden floor. I shared the couch with Daedalus, who looked more Husky than German Shepherd. He watched her with mild interest, his blue eyes like cool oases in the humid afternoon. Her footsteps reminded me of Rorschach inkblots and I interpreted: fear, extreme impatience. Hers, not mine. I felt as porous as a sea sponge, everything drifting through me, leaving barely a trace.

She bent over me, her spare frame rattling with anger. "What are you doing? Your daughter is falling apart while you sit here lost in space. What are you thinking, Sophie?"

My father walked out of the kitchen. "Why did you say that, Janice? Thomas just drowned! Good grief—she's in shock!"

"Why don't you talk to her then?"

He slipped out the front screen door, his glance full of tender anxiety.

I pressed deeper into the couch, but held my hands out to her. She turned toward my mother, who sat in the shadowy kitchen. My silence had transformed me from a grieving widow deserving of gentleness to a person made monstrous by inexplicable behavior: I did not join in the collective keening. I counted Janice's footsteps from the front door to the kitchen to the living room—thirty-one, but more as she retraced her steps now. Her chestnut hair swung at her shoulders. I wanted to tell her it was a good cut, it brought out her deep-set eyes. Weariness made her beautiful skin look papery, almost fragile.

"Nothing will go away because you won't talk." She slumped into the chair opposite me. "It's been eleven days now. Thomas is buried, the family is exhausted, and we have to leave tomorrow. I can understand your not wanting to talk much to mom and dad yet, or Galen and Michael. Even our brothers gave up and retreated! I know you're devastated, Sophie…but this is me asking you to come back…." Tears rounded her words. Strands of hair stuck to her damp cheeks.

Out of the corner of my eye I could see my adolescent daughter slowly descend the spiral stairway and then sit on the bottom step. Mia wore the same thing she had at the funeral—a black tank top and a short black skirt from which her coltish legs emerged. I wondered if she had worn these every day. She stared at me until I met her eyes, and they were swollen from weeping, damaged by sleeplessness. I heard her get up the nights I lay cocooned between sleep and wakefulness, waited for the bending of her knees against the backs of mine. Once she had returned to me, I would sleep another hour or two, the sound of her breathing like the lull of the sea. But no words were exchanged, only her circular questions—why/how could he/what will we do—that I could not answer.

I stroked Dae's head, found a burr, and tugged at it gently. He pulled away and sniffed the air, licked my chin roughly, and watched me watching him. He had more sense than my family. He knew how to wait, when to seek me out, when to leave me to my own devices. I wondered if he would return to me when I couldn't call his name. I had an impulse to try to outstare him. He panted lightly, then looked away.

Janice got up and went to Mia, speaking softly. Mia loved her; she had missed Janice and her twelve-year-old cousin, Lilly, more than the rest of the family. She'd told me this when we moved here only months before. I'd expected her to name my mother, who doted on her for being the first-born grandchild, sending her care packages of cookies and ten dollar checks, books and gift certificates for clothes. She spent two weeks with my parents every year when school was out in June. Not this year. We had fallen through a trapdoor and who knew where we would land?

What is it that you want? I asked Janice, but of course I wasn't heard. Do you need great outbursts, tearing of my hair? I had sat stunned on the deck every day until Thomas was lowered into the ground in Haston's Place of Peace Cemetery and felt the tears flood my mouth, salty trails crisscrossing my skin like a web. I remember not being able to breathe. I studied the squat circle of land an eighth mile from the shore that Thomas, a biologist specializing in limnology, had wanted to make his own. I imagined him walking its breadth, muttering about the ungodly price of paradise and the ignorance of people who polluted the waters with outboard motors and set up colonies of two-legged omnivores on the eroding banks. He said these things with the disgust born of a superior mind tolerating the dominion of the majority. He wanted to build a tiny one-room cabin on the island for long hours of research, bottles of waters cloudy with the detritus of invisible life forms. I believe he might have ended up living there, returning to the chapel-house on weekends for our nurturance, random laughter, food. For my mouth, which he tenderly outlined with his fingertip.

I remembered him shouting excitedly when he ran down to the shore the minute the sales contract for the house was signed, how he stood on the end of the peninsula and then turned a full circle, hands outstretched. "All mine!" he bellowed. Then, tossed over his shoulder: "Ours, Sophie!"

I remembered his hand on my back as we drowsed in the clean sunlight the last morning we awakened together, the musky smell of his breath, the roughness of his callused feet on my calves.

His last morning greeting, "Arise, celestial Sophia." Was it tinged with disdain or was he still hoping there was immeasurable love at hand?

I remembered the afternoon and evening before he drowned and then the memories darkened dangerously like smoke. There was no other side, no way out. I crawled like a coward and when I tried to call for help, out rushed silence instead. Too late. He was gone.

What else should I do? I asked Janice and willed her to hear me. I had signed all the documents, picked out his casket, watched the loamy earth pile on top of it. Behind me had stood four of Thomas' colleagues and oldest friends including his office mate. It was he who had most warned Thomas against leaving the university, and his face was pale and damp, his eyes narrowed with sadness and embarrassed guilt, as though his prophecy of Thomas' demise had made it so. I heard someone ask his mother why Thomas wasn't buried in Boston, and the answer was short: "He left a diary. This was his wish." The diary was really a loose-leaf notebook that was full of data as well as odd jottings of his feelings, impressions, plans. Near the middle, at the bottom of the page of quick sketches of the vegetation on the island, he wrote, "*I feel as though I have found a habitation I want to never leave, the village I have come to recognize as a real home in so short a time. I have all that I need at last. I would pray if I could muster a facsimile of belief—but for that, I have Sophie.*"

I knelt there a long while, my family murmuring around me, Mia folded in the curve of my arms. My father's hand never left my shoulder; my mother's eyes examined the contours of my face. What did they see? Nothing but mindless sorrow. My arch rival brothers, Michael and Galen, sang a mourning song, an Irish dirge, their incompatible voices entwined without argument this one time. My mother-in-law, Vita Swanson, hobbled toward me in a black suit and length of pearls, kissed the heavy air around my head. Her perfume made my stomach lurch, gardenia, a ruined richness. I thought of Thomas' cousins, how they couldn't make it, being in Europe on business; how he had no siblings to answer the mourning call. His aunts and uncles were either dead or too aged to travel.

"He should have stayed where he belonged," Vita said, "in Vermont or Boston. He could have had the house and acreage in the White Mountains if he would have just asked before Robert passed on! You could have been happy there. He didn't have to work this long or hard, for God's sake. What was he trying to prove? Buying an old chapel and pretending it was a rustic home! And now this—buried in foreign ground! It was always his way, wasn't it? Bull-headedness killed my husband, and now my son!" She dabbed her rheumy eyes with a linen handkerchief and patted me on the back. "If there's anything I can do… I know Thomas provided well for you but, still, you know I am here…" A sharp cry was muffled with her handkerchief and then she straightened up. "Mia? Come here, honey."

But Mia had left with Lilly, swinging her cousin's hand in a slow, wide arc, her head hanging, her feet dragging in the dirt. Vita crumpled in my mother's arms, at last more bereft than angry. I watched from a distance, seeing their disarrayed emotions, their disbelief. Death would be equated with Vita Swanson's extravagant scent for the rest of my life.

What sort of mother had she been to my husband? They netted each other with demands and promises. There was an absence of sweetness. And Robert, his father? His plane went down over Grand Cayman Islands, at the edge of a hurricane. Dauntless, unsentimental, powerful, and dead at sixty-eight. I wanted to tell her I was sorry for everything. But then thought: dangerous, foolish Swansons. She left the next morning and I wept. It was the shape of her hands and fingers as they held mine when she said good-bye: Thomas's hands, only smaller, smoother, and warm. She pressed her cheek to mine and I felt loneliness like a rawness that didn't heal.

My family convened on the deck overlooking the lake. What to do with Sophie? This was the main topic since Thomas' funeral. They spoke of me as though I was eavesdropping, their intentions sheltered in softened tones that, from my place in the gazebo, I could easily interpret. They hunched over the round table a few feet from me, the shadow from the umbrella giving their faces a dusky pallor.

"She should come home," my father said.

"She won't live with us," my mother stated flatly once more.

"Sophie hasn't done hard physical labor in thirty years. She's out here in the backwoods!"

"Oh, she's a strong girl. She's a dancer, remember? She can't talk, Lucas! That's the problem here."

"Who says it's a problem? She needs time, that's all."

My mother sighed, and reached for my father's hand.

Janice looked toward me. "Let's drop the idea of her moving any time soon. What is most important is that she gets the help she needs so Mia can stay—"

"Mia can't stay! Sophie can't stand shrinks." My father shuddered, nodding in assent.

"Let's figure out how Mia can stay here. I was thinking of the computer Sophie put in the garage a few days ago. We need her to use it, like Galen and Michael said, so she can at least communicate that way. Mia, too."

177

My mother shook her head. "If she wanted to use it, she wouldn't have put it away. It was Thomas'. Everything of his has already been stored or given away. Like she's banished him!" She dabbed away tears.

"Maybe she'll use it later. Until then, there's the mail, the phone…well, Mia can call us or whoever she needs, can't she?" Janice stood up and walked toward me, then turned back to our parents. "Maybe it's like a safety zone. It's not that unusual for people in shock to go mute."

"I saw it during the war," my father began. Mother shushed him.

Yes. A safety zone. A moat. Or maybe a curse has descended. None of you is invited in until it is lifted. Be gone! I faced Ring Lake and watched Mia sitting on the beach. She jumped up and turned as though she felt my eyes on her, waved half-heartedly, and walked slowly along the shore. She looked like a waif, her black tank top barely covering her waist, feet bare, long hair straggling into her face as she kicked the sand with each step. She had become angular, less than herself, and part of me wanted to run to her and grab her and hold her so close she would beat me off. But the other part—the enraged woman who had just lost an entire life—thought of leaving her behind, and goosebumps rose along my neck and arms.

I walked over to the table where they sat, unable to solve this conundrum of sister and daughter bereft of the spoken word. I slapped my hands flat on the warm glass surface. Their eyes lifted in concert. I pressed my hands sharply against the bee-humming air and their words and then left them to join Mia. If sound had come, I would have said: "Leave us alone. We're still breathing. Stop trying to imagine what we have or what we need!" Or I might have screamed, vivid waves of sound piercing the beauty of the north country.

Every day since the drowning there had been no peace. Mouths eating the air like ravenous things. Sleep in one-hour stretches, drugged, damp, empty. Mia and I wrapped in a thin white blanket on the bed. She felt so heavy at first, then frail, as though each minute took her further from me, a phantom fleeing. I strove to speak her name but only the heat of my breath covered her closed eyes. She began to recede, to turn her back on me. She found solace in the drone of words traded with the others while I sank into this urn of muteness. Death left me behind, and I tracked trails of heat left by the living.

Shaking out my waist-length, ginger-white hair, I ran to the beach and blindly stumbled over my daughter's legs, falling into the water and her shriek.

"Mother! I hate this! You're acting demented!"

I looked up and saw Mia and my family in chiaroscuro: life reduced to a minimum against an electric summer sky.

I held my breath, dove deep below, captive in clothing that belonged to another woman who stole my voice, which once tethered me to the ones I loved. You never know when speaking just one word might save you.

Another day: the stand-off as we huddled on the couch.

"Mom, they won't let me stay here if you don't talk."

I touched her hand, and she grabbed mine in both of hers until my fingers ached.

"I want to stay, but…." She sounded hoarse and whispery and I wanted to tell her to speak up, don't mumble. "I'm scared." She began to shake a little, the boney knee next to mine vibrating, and I put my arm around her, pulled her head to my chest, and her hot tears trickled down my chest. "You can't just shut us all out…you can't leave me now that daddy's gone. I don't know what to do anymore." She sat up and yelled in a porridge-y voice, "Stop doing this to us!"

Her wide mouth opened and shut, full, then empty. Eyes a dense blue like the heart of flame. She took my arms in her strong hands and shook me and Dae barked in alarm. I could have stood up and pulled her to me, her bruising sorrow engulfed in my six foot motherness. I might have begged her to stay, but why drag her with me into hell? So, nothing. Her rage must have jumped into me because as Janice led her outside, I grabbed the daisies atop the mantel and dumped them into the fireplace. Then I picked up each pot of sympathy and threw them in as well, crockery breaking at my feet, the sterilized earth an avalanche on the Persian carpet. Note cards from old friends fell open and their words of regret vanished in damp dirt and broken pieces.

Mia's fingerprints stayed with me, each red streak a mark of my failure to provide her safety from the unexpected. I could almost taste her language and found it sour and heavy. I got up and drank water from the kitchen faucet's cool stream a long time, but my throat still burned. I went to bed, Dae slinking behind me, and I thought for a moment he might speak, but he did not.

The next morning they left for Vermont as I lay on the bed staring out the skylight at the bland sky. First my parents, then Janice, with hands smoothing my hair and then forehead as though it was feverish.

"We'll come back any time you want, Sophia," my mother said.

"Yes. If it wasn't for your mother's diabetes acting up... " My father's voice was a low rumble.

I smiled at them and sat up. Tears ran down my face as though someone had drilled a hole deep inside, struck water, liberated rivulets from a hidden place. I put my arms around them and then they melted into the dust-filled sunlight of the doorway.

Mia stood where they had just passed, her suitcases in each hand.

"I'm coming back soon, mom. I'll call you this weekend when I get settled at Aunt Janice's, but you have to answer and listen, okay? Do what you have to do so I can come home, mom. If you don't stop this I don't know if I can stand it. Mom! Mom?"

Her voice was so clear it hurt, glass shattering on a cement floor. She kissed me on the cheek. Such heat in her, her life pushing against this barrier of grief. She backed away, then turned and disappeared.

I lay down and watched the circling of birds above me, the loft of the wind setting their wings at angles to the square of sky. It all fit in that window: sky winking, feathers sailing, sun drained of color. A blue jay gave warning and I turned my head at the sound of the front door slamming shut. My lips formed her name. Then the chapel-house closed around me and I felt its long life in the wooden floors, the rafters, the thick, winter-ready walls.

Why did they pray here, in this aged chapel ruined by us? To ease pain? To illuminate perfect love? I could not remember what such steadfast belief or boundless forgiveness meant. But I did remember the Bible story about King Solomon and an infant fought over by two women, each claiming to be the mother. Solomon told them he would divide the child in two so each would be satisfied. He knew the real mother would make herself known and she did. She gave up the child to the other woman in order to save her son's life.

I gave Mia to my sister because it was her chance of survival. If she had seen me falter, imagined there was something I kept from her, she would not have walked out that door and in the end I would have lost her.

It was no mistake that I was born both strong and agile of body and soul. They think I am sleepwalking through widowhood, but I am conserving my energies. I let Mia go so that I can prepare for battle with the demon who wore the face of my husband the night he died.

Pobrecito Pavo

Patty Clement

"You're here! You're here! Go meet the Thanksgiving turkey!" cry the teachers when my daughter and I arrive at her school. That sounds so cute: I imagine shaking a bare, frozen drumstick. Thanksgiving is our favorite holiday and I've come to share it with my daughter, the International Coordinator of a Spanish immersion school in Quetzaltenengo, Guatemala.

We feel special, extended this cross-cultural gift. The teachers searched several markets before locating the turkey. One of the school administrators called my daughter, Katie, this morning and excitedly told her they'd finally located one.

"They've never celebrated Thanksgiving at Escuela Pop Wuj before," Katie says with a hint of a smile.

We stroll toward the kitchen, but our walk ends in the little indoor courtyard. At our feet the turkey paces in a tight circle, tethered to the leg of the sink. He is so skinny that I can almost see the bones protrude through his bedraggled, dull feathers. His gaze darts around the room and every few seconds he emits a piercing, grating "eeeek."

I give the turkey a wide berth. Who knows if turkeys attack humans or what damage his sharp yellow beak and curved little claws could do? Katie and I exchange a wary glance. Who is expected to kill, clean and cook this fowl? Our gift may have come with consequences.

"Thank you so much," Katie and I say in unison. But I hear a hollow ring to our words. The teachers are laughing.

"We're looking forward to Thanksgiving dinner!" they call as they leave the room. I scroll through my memory, trying to retrieve a recipe and a method to cook a live turkey.

"Momma," Katie says, "Amalia wants to cook the turkey." I want to throw my arms around Amalia, I'm so grateful that I don't have to touch that bird until it's cooked.

"But she wants someone else to kill it first," Katie adds. So I'm not quite relieved of all responsibility yet.

Luis, my teacher, joins us in the courtyard. I am visiting Katie for a month and have taken two days of a four-week course of individual Spanish lessons. Katie, using a perk of her position, assigned me the best teacher in the school. I admire the ease with which he stands well within pecking distance of the turkey. He smiles broadly and seems amused by our discomfort. I am sure he knows this is the first time I have looked Thanksgiving dinner in the eye.

Luis motions to me to follow him and I gladly leave the turkey behind. We settle in at our little table.

"Tell me the significance of your Thanksgiving," Luis says.

"After the first harvest in America the settlers invited the Native Americans to a big celebration to give thanks that they survived the winter." I stop abruptly, picturing the scenario from Luis' perspective. His Mayan ancestors lived for thousands of years in Central America before the conquistadors and the passengers on the Mayflower arrived in the Americas. Luis is Ladino, the product of the race of the Spanish conquistadors mixing with the Mayan Indians in Guatemala. I feel the warmth rise in my face and I pitch another of my naïve ethnocentric beliefs into the growing pile of discarded, shameful attitudes. It's been thirty-five years since I've visited a developing country. As a student, I hitchhiked across Muslim Morocco and was brought to my senses when my hitchhiking partner was offered two camels in trade for me. In the intervening years I'd thought I'd honed my cultural sensitivity, but now I'm not so sure. I begin again.

"It's a harvest celebration." He nods. Silence stretches between us.

Luis speaks first. "Let's begin our lesson. The first day we learned the verb for the temporary state of 'to be,' estar. Today we will learn ser, the word denoting the permanent state of being."

The distinction in the Spanish language between the temporary and permanent states of being amused and engaged me two days ago, but today every fifteen seconds my attention is disrupted by a gobble-shriek. After the thirtieth gobble I decide you can hear fear in the shriek.

The gobbles suddenly increase in volume and frequency. Katie bursts through the door leading the turkey by his leash, with several students following her. She marches through our room, takes a hard right into the computer room and walks straight into a small indoor courtyard, a little larger than the one next to the kitchen. The courtyard shares a wall with our room, with a large window punched in it. We can only see the top third of Katie and the rest of the occupants. We can't tell exactly what they are doing, with the lower part of their bodies hidden.

"I need a knife!" Katie's disembodied voice calls out.

"Probecito pavo," comments Luis and he fakes a look of concern. The poor little turkey begins to gobble continuously. I feel anxious too, aware that until recently Katie has been a vegetarian and that it appears she's been delegated to kill this bird. Excited students walk through our room and gather to watch in the small courtyard with the overflow along the window in our room. We hear a scuffle. Luis jumps up and rushes in to help. My stomach begins to roll. The energy of the crowd pulls me towards the window, but I don't want to join them. I do not want to see what Katie is doing on the other side of the wall.

Fredy, the Guatemalan administrator who shares an office with Katie, walks in and looks over at me, sitting alone at my little desk. I have wanted to thank him for his kind treatment of my daughter, but have been unable to because he maintains that embarrassment keeps him from speaking English.

"You aren't going to watch this, are you?" Fredy asks me in perfect, unaccented English. So much for his embarrassment. I take his question as my permission to leave the room and go to the kitchen to pace and wait out the slaughter.

After an interminable time Katie, her face pale and expressionless, comes into the kitchen.

"It's done," she says simply. She washes the knife under the running water in the sink, then carefully dries it.

"Are you okay, Katie?" I can hardly believe that my daughter, who wrote a passionate college application essay on the ethics of killing and autopsying laboratory rats in the quest for a cure for breast cancer, just killed a turkey.

"Of course I am, Momma," she says. Katie prides herself on her toughness.

I ask, "Why did you have to lead the effort to kill the turkey?" I'm indignant for her.

"I am going to eat it, so I thought I should help kill it too." I stare at my daughter. How often does a mother witness a defining moment of character growth in their child? I mark for myself another privilege of this trip.

Luis joins us in the kitchen, calmly washes his hands, and returns to our study table. His manner is casual, no taint of murder surrounding him.

"We will try again to speak of the verb for the temporal 'to be'," Luis says. I'm not up to declining a verb right now. I can't act like nothing untoward happened in the adjoining room.

My mind riffs on the temporal and permanent states of being. This first experience of the thin Guatemalan membrane between a beating heart and a still one burrows into my psyche.

The mystical Thanksgiving turkey, the one that struts in my childhood imagination with a rainbow of feathers arcing behind it like a peacock's tail, passed through my room a mere ten minutes ago, bristling with energy, drawing the entire school behind in its wake. Now it resides ignobly in the kitchen sink, perfectly motionless, its detached feathers creating a mound of soft fluff on the floor, exposing the soft, pink flesh underneath. Whether we admit it or not, we all reside in the temporary state of being. Whether turkey or human, Guatemalan or North American, we are all impermanent, here for a brief shining moment to strut our stuff. And then, in a blink, we vanish.

Log Song

Amy Minato

Fire, the lover, places its cape
of flame around your trunk
tongues toward heartwood.
Seared leaves scatter to mulch.

You cannot move but
tremble slightly, remembering
this could happen.

Wind like a stranger
standing too close pushes,
pushes until you lean

beyond balance, split
at center and begin
your slow fall to earth.

Bark beetles slip
beneath charred sheaths
place eggs shining with fungi
spore for their larvae to eat
as they scrape veins
in the underside of bark. In time

your trunk will collapse
into soil, while seedlings
rise from deep layers

of moss and small mammals
trespass your cavity. You
are soft rot inhabited
by uninvited life, soggy
sorrowing, inseparable
from earth itself, the loam
the humus, the way back.

Morning

Miriam Feder

Awaken spirit
Speak the smallest grains of truth
Boulders will follow

Dance of the Thunder Gods

Melissa C. Reardon

The clouds had been floating gently across the sky all day. Some were stretched to their limit, others were small and puffy. They gave up no raindrops as they sailed across the vibrant blue skies. Yet the birds chirped in the ponderosas, chipmunks scuttled across the pine forest floor and lizards languished on the cool rocks along the creek banks. A slight cooling breeze began to lift the branches of the trees and gently coaxed the grass sideways, but when it ceased, the heavy heat rested again upon the earth. As the hot day plodded along, the air became listless, oppressive, even suffocating. Except for the breeze playing about in the tree tops and the quiet chuckling of the creek, the day became silent and still.

By the end of the afternoon, the clouds had flourished, blossoming in the hot humid sky. Growing slowly, they merged with each other, becoming swollen stanchions of steam and energy, blocking their blue background. Cloudy hands grasped at each other under the forging towers of thunderheads. The setting sun flickered among the clouds bringing hues of rusts, reds and purples to their heavenly underbellies. Color was flung across the sky in the death throes of the day while the earth waited. Then the air no longer stirred, but became so dense, it felt as if it could be cut into tiny pieces.

With the very last rays of sunlight, the air began to move in strong short bursts, whirling dust into tiny parched tornadoes that blew helpless tumbleweeds across the sagebrush landscape. Distant rumblings could be heard in the darkening horizon as the sky turned from gray to starless black. Flashes of light danced across the turbulent skyline, illuminating the large silhouettes of painted hills as they stood fast against the storm. Moving closer, its energy crackled across the desert.

The atmosphere was broken by large raindrops—plopping into the dust, breaking onto sun warmed rocks, slapping the leaves of the evening primrose while it rolled down the stalks of desert sage. The black sky exploded with dangerous powerful fingers of thunderbolts as they reached across the lake and pronounced their warning of the storm's inevitable approach.

The air swirled about the oak groves, while menacing tendrils of electricity grabbed the sky in both desperation and domination, turning the evening clouds an eerie pink, purple and gray. And the earth trembled beneath them. Thunder rattled and boomed its war cry and the lightning just kept on dancing to its music. Rain poured down from the heavens, saturating the thirsty soil, quenching its late summer thirst as small rivulets of storm water moved down the withered hills. Ozone and sulphur filled the air with a mystical aroma, mingling with the refreshing scent of wet lava rock, white sage and cleansing juniper.

The storm moved slowly across the beaten skyline for what seemed like hours, demanding full attention, always threatening instant destruction. After an earth-shattering boom, a flickering tentacle touched a pine tree, instantly setting it aflame. Fire danced back along the tentacle's course, lighting up the hillside. The tempest moved on to pummel against a mountain range, looming in the distance. As it took its leave, flickers of light faded beyond the horizon, thunder became just quiet muttering and then there was silence. The clouds parted to reveal the sparkling stars of the clean evening sky while the owl made its stealthy journey through the pine trees to start his evening hunt...as if nothing had ever happened at all.

On May 21st, 2006

Carol Ellis

they took down the cooling tower at Trojan.
A crowd watched at seven a.m. as the whole thing collapsed.
The spent fuel remains, waste that will need storage
for ten thousand years.

How do you think about time like that? We live at most a hundred.
For thousands of years it will be someone's job to remember the stored waste
of nuclear fission, where it lies and how it's kept in some final cavern.
Will they pass it down generations, a caste of watchers?

Whole worlds can be forgotten and reformed in that time. In our arrogance
we've created this duty for unseen descendants, the whole race of humans tied.
Perhaps it will be religion, holy sites barred, protected by priests of radiation past,
or forgotten, stumbled on after many wars—
a living reminder, a final gift.

peace march, 2/16/03
— for Carol

Deborah Akers

soap bubbles blown
by a child riding
high shoulders

disperse in the crowd
like a galaxy of frail
planets lacking a sun

they light on passing
backs and necks
balance on

unknowing heads
before gently shattering
into faint, wet

unfelt blessings

one lands in the crook
of my arm
I slow a bit, cradling

the weightless globe
for a few brief steps
before it tears away

lost in the wake
of the human stream

Deborah Akers live in Portland, OR—a recent return to the Pacific Northwest from the sunny salt mines of California. Portland is for her a dynamic sanctuary, a sylvan bower set square in the world. She makes her living as an educational writer.

Tiel Aisha Ansari is a Sufi, martial artist, and computer programmer living in Portland, OR, where she works for the public school district. Her poetry has appeared in *Islamica Magazine* and *Barefoot Muse* and is forthcoming in *Mythic Delirium* and *Shit Creek Review,* among others. She recently won the Iron Poet Bouts-Rimes award given at Westercon 60.

When **Katherina Audley** is not at work in her art studio in North Portland, she trots the globe in search of large marine mammals to play with, cultural illnesses to be afflicted by and big fish to kill and eat. Katherina also enjoys amassing enormous bodies of data for use in her pseudoscientific art projects. Someday, she hopes to have a dog and a garden. To find out more, visit: www.kpetunia.com.

Kristina Bak writes, paints, teaches Essence Qigong, and does Energy-harmonizing healing in Bend, Oregon. Her work has been published in the U.S., Finland, and in Australia, her second home.

Jo Barney is retired and has spent the past ten years doing what she's been dreaming of doing all of her life: reading and writing. Her essays and short stories have appeared in small literary magazines, anthologies and on the web. One publication, the *Reader's Digest,* even paid her for her efforts. From that check on, years ago, her resume and tax report have read: Writer. She finds it intriguing that her stories used to be about young and middle-aged women. Now many of her characters have developed age spots and large capacities for reminiscing about old boyfriends.

Barbara E. Berger has lived in Portland, Oregon since 1974. She periodically visits her native New York, keeping family connections strong and her Bronx accent fresh. Barbara has more than 20 years experience working for the state of Oregon, focusing on government writing. Her book reviews and author interviews have appeared in *El Hispanic News.* Barbara is a Civil Tongues Toastmaster Club officer, and she sings alto with the Neveh Shalom Choir.

Kristin Berger's poetry and non-fiction has appeared in *The American Poetry Journal, The Comstock Review, Pilgrimage* and online at *Mamazine, Her Circle E-zine, Hip Mama, Hot Metal Press* and other journals. She live in Portland with her husband, daughter and son. This year finds Kristin growing vegetables and babies, piecing quilts, plotting poems and elaborating grand essays. Her collection of poems, *For the Willing,* will be available from Finishing Line Press in 2007/2008.

Marina Braun has called Portland, OR home for eighteen years since she immigrated to the United States from Russia. She teaches courses in translation at Portland State University and devotes her spare time to writing (in English and Russian).

AnnCary moved to Portland a year ago, convinced it would be a good fit since her longstanding favorite color is gray. Despite her wandering roots, she's fallen in love with the Northwest and intends to make it home with her partner, Kelly, and dog, Lea. She enjoys berry picking, camping, ice cream making, swimming, cross country skiing and making truffles.

Stacy Carleton believes that we all have a place in the community of writers. When she is not training for her Jazzercise instructor license, making up fake DJ names, dreaming of a post-ironic world in which sincerity and enthusiasm are cool again, or falling off a surfboard on the Oregon coast, she teaches high school language arts. She lives in northeast Portland.

Rachael Cate is a writer living in Portland, Oregon. She has published poetry, fiction and nonfiction articles which explore a consciousness of identities, environments, and relationships. Her poem "Hunger Pangs" recently received Declaration Editing's *Four and Twenty Short Form Poetry Contest* award. She tours the United States by bicycle, sometimes riding 1,000 miles to achieve authentic accounts of the land. She is currently an associate editor at *The Bear Deluxe* magazine.

Patty Clement has worked in social services for many years and has published in venues as disparate as the *Journal of Prevention, Transitions Abroad* and *American Bungalow Magazine.* One of her nonfiction stories earned an honorable mention award from the Oregon Writers Colony. "Pobrecito Pavo" is an excerpt from her memoir, *Breaking the Surface.*

Helen Crowley Cheek is spending her retirement years pursuing diverse interests postponed since childhood. She has been published in *The Sun, Portland, The Oregonian* and *On Point, the Magazine of the U. S. Army Museum.* She won first prize for non-fiction in Marylhurst University's *M Review* literary contest in 2006. Her eight children are grateful that she doesn't write about them.

Sage Cohen's writing appears in more than 30 journals and anthologies including *Poetry Flash, Oregon Literary Review, blueoregon.com* and *San Francisco Reader*. In 2006, she won first prize in Ghost Road Press' annual poetry contest. Sage holds a MA in creative writing from New York University where she was awarded a *New York Times* fellowship. She has taught poetry at universities, hospitals, writing conferences and online. Visit Sage at www.sagesaidso.com.

Caren Coté was shaken from the San Francisco Bay Area in 1989. She's lived in and around Portland, Oregon ever since, where she belongs, and works in the Silicon Forest to support her writing habit, her cat Phoebe, and various local garden centers. She's currently polishing a novel.

Virginia Davis was born in 1942 in South Carolina and raised in Alaska, France and northern California. She has a B.A. in History from Reed College and an M.A. in English (Poetry) from San Francisco State. In 1979 she returned to Portland to live and in 1992 published Anima Speaking, a collection of poems. Louise Bogan and Robert Creeley are major influences. These days she writes the occasional poem and paints.

Carol Ellis lives in Forest Grove, OR with her husband. They have two grown children, and the requisite dog and cat. She is a graduate of Reed College and works as a psychiatric nurse in Portland. In the early 1970s she was active in the womens movement in Portland, and has a special affection for womens poetry and womens publications. Her work has appeared in *Windfall* and *Fireweed* magazines.

Diane English retired from her first life and moved to Portland to write after a second bout with cancer. "Coming Clean" comes from a writing group prompt, part of the story of recovery she describes in her memoir, *Private Poet: A Healing Journey*. Diane attributes her return to health—in body, mind, and spirit—to writing the poems and stories of her life, guided and supported by Portland's wonderful community of writers. She's been cancer-free for over a decade now.

Miriam Feder debuted *The Vestibule*, her first one-woman show, at HipBone Studio in June. Miriam has written for work and pleasure throughout her life, including two musicals for student performance (*In Portland* and *Even To The Western Ocean*) and the work that feeds her performances and weekly podcast habit. Check out more at miriamfeder.com.

Jane Galin lives in Portland, Oregon.

Shanna Germain spends as much time as possible in her home office dreaming up words and worlds. Her award-winning poems, short stories and essays have been published in places like *Absinthe Literary Review, the American Journal of Nursing, Best American Erotica 2007, Best Gay Romance 2008, Salon* and *Tattoo Highway.* Visit her at www.shannagermain.com.

Heidi Schulman Greenwald lives in Portland, OR with her husband and two children. She spent ten years pursuing a career in writing, editing and strategic communication, and her business work has been published in a variety of print and online publications. As a stay-at-home mom, she now spends her free time taming her backyard forest, practicing her headstands, and writing poetry.

Sara Guest is a midwesterner by birth and breeding, a northwesterner in temperament. An editor by trade, she works as a program coordinator for Write Around Portland and volunteers for other local writing organizations, including Literary Arts, The Northwest Writing Institute and (of course) VoiceCatcher.

Doris Hammons is a writer from Portland, Oregon.

Allegra Heidelinde lives in Portland, Oregon. Raised in Taos, New Mexico, she also calls Santa Barbara, California home. A lifelong lover of the classical and expressive arts, she now teaches the Feldenkrais Method of somatic education. Jokes, poetry, and love letters for her cat may be sent to aheidelinde@yahoo.com.

Elizabeth Jones' background is in creative direction, performance, and earthbody love. She lives in a magic house with many friends, 4 chickens, and a dog. She is co-director of Bodies in Balance, a Pilates studio and mind-body integration site.

Frances Kiva moved to the Pacific Northwest fifteen years ago from Southern California because she thought the weather would be better. She now lives in Portland, OR with her two daughters and an ancient, white dog that sheds copious amounts of fur.

Jennifer Lalime, editor of VoiceCatcher 2007, is a northwest native, a writer, a mother, a wife, and a workshop leader with Portland Women Writers.

Lori Maliszewski spent over twenty years working in high-tech marketing, all the while searching for the perfect cup of coffee. Her work has appeared in the anthologies: *How to Leave a Place* and *Cup of Comfort for Writers*. Her memoir, *Cancer a Love Story,* chronicles the three years following a diagnosis with incurable cancer. She will self-publish it the summer of 2007. She lives in Portland, Oregon with her husband, Steve.

Amy Minato is author of *The Wider Lens* published in 2004 by Ice River Press. Her poetry has been widely published and recognized with a 2003 Oregon Literary Arts Fellowship and her prose with a Walden Fellowship. She currently teaches poetry writing at Washington State University in Vancouver, creative writing in Portland schools, and writing workshops around the region. She lives with her husband and two children in Portland and migrates in summer to the Wallowa Mountains.

Melanie Springer Mock is mother to two five-year-old boys. When not picking up dirty socks or stepping over Legos, she works as an associate professor of writing and literature at George Fox University, Newberg, Oregon. Her work has been published in *Adoptive Families, Literary Mama, The Chronicle of Higher Education*, and *Brain, Child*, among other places. Her book, *Writing Peace: The Unheard Voices of Great War Mennonite Objectors*, was published by Cascadia in 2003.

A native Oregonian, **Gwendolyn Morgan** has commuted by bicycle to work for over a decade. Her poetry is published in: *Calyx, Kalliope*, and other literary journals. With much gratitude to her mentors, she holds an MFA in Creative Writing from Goddard College and an MDiv from San Francisco Theological Seminary. She has been a recipient of writing residencies at Caldera and Soapstone. Gwendolyn and her partner share their home with Boone, an Australian Cattledog.

Richelle Morgan is a writer specializing in fundraising letters for non-profit organizations, website copy and short feature articles. She lives in Portland, Oregon with her husband and three small children, who are kind enough to allow her time to work on the second draft of her first novel and other fiction projects.

Lee Haas Norris moved to Portland, Oregon from Portland, Maine four years ago. She has published travel stories in *The Boston Globe* and *The Washington Post*, and personal essays in *The New York Times, Maine Times, Wolf Moon Press Journal*, and the on-line magazines *Mamazine* and *Common Ties*. She plays in a Renaissance recorder group, is an English Country dancer, and is participating for the fourth year in the Portland Christmas Revels.

Paulann Petersen's work has appeared in *Poetry, The New Republic, Prairie Schooner, Willow Springs, Calyx,* and the *Internet's Poetry Daily.* Collections of her poems include *The Wide Awake* (Confluence Press, 2002); *Blood Silk* (Quiet Lion Press, 2004); and *A Bride of Narrow Escape* (Cloudbank Books, 2006). A former Stegner Fellow at Stanford University, she serves on the board of Friends of William Stafford, organizing the January Stafford Birthday Events.

Susan Prindle is or has been a wife, mother, grandmother of 5, hospital clown, pilot, Californian, hang-glider (only once!), lifeguard, barista, antique dealer, rock climber (also only once), not-often-enough writer and a volunteer naturalist. She has lived in Portland now for 11 years and misses the sun. At the present moment she is practicing learning to be happy just as she is.

Jenette Purcell loves to sit amid her splendid collection of "see no evil, speak no evil, hear no evil" monkeys, after which she ruminates on the pain and pleasure found in the perfect poem. Otherwise, she can be seen regaling Portland with her self-tailored savoir-faire and joie de vivre at art events, restaurants and cemeteries. She can also be read in books throughout North America.

Melissa C. Reardon is an Oregon native (one of the few left from the old *granola* days). She tends to her organic veggie garden, plays soccer with her border collie, meets with her regular writing groups and loves to go camping with her husband. She plays Celtic and Classical music, teaches creatives how to market their work and writes when her dog will let her. She spends her free time volunteering and promoting sustainability.

Cynthia Richardson lives in Portland, OR and is a chemical dependency clinician. She writes fiction, poetry, non-fiction, and occasionally lyrics. She is fortunate to have mothered five children and now enjoys their children.

Sandra Sakurai thinks of poetry as wearable art, one which expresses memories, amusement and musings which she enjoys reading aloud. A mid-westerner who came to Oregon in 2000 via Maryland, she lives with her family in Troutdale letting Whimsyko and Greyson in and out, reading, writing, painting watercolors and frying crayons to make art. She has studied with Paulann Peterson and David Biespiel.

Lilian Sarlos is a mama, teacher and at long last a writer in Portland. Her work has appeared in *Motherverse, Mother Earth News, Southeast Examiner,* and *Teachers Always Write.* She is trying her hand at a novel for pre-teens. In the occasional lull she seeks the divine in the beautiful family and numerous critters in her home/circus.

Heidi Schmaltz is a Portland native mainly of Scandinavian and German descent. She is newly married to a man from Holguin, Cuba. She has traveled extensively in South America, is fluent in Spanish and works in the language interpretation field. Starting in the fall of '07 she will be pursuing her Master's degree in Spanish as well as teaching the language at Portland State University, where she also received her Bachelor's degree in Anthropology. She can be contacted at heidi.astrid@gmail.com.

Amanda Sledz is (or has been) a journalist, literary magazine editor (and contributor), grant writer, advice columnist, serial blogger, and comic book scholar. Both her memoir *300 Feet Tall*, and her novel *Psychopomp* will be completed by April 2008. Amanda grew up in Cleveland before catapulting to Portland, where she now lives with two wonderful cats that refuse to pull her in a chariot, and lots of humans who join her in bike-riding decadence.

Gerri Ravyn Stanfield practices acupuncture and aikido in the lush Willamette river valley. Originally a Kentucky native, she has finally made a nest in Portland, Oregon. She is a writer, teacher, lover, artist and activist dedicated to coaxing more magic into the world through the cracks in modern culture. Gerri can be found at: www.forestspringacupuncture.com.

Kristin Steele lives and writes in North Portland. She completed her MFA in creative writing at Goddard College. Her work has appeared in *Curve*, *Outlook*, and the anthology *Love Shook My Heart II* as well as online at *Logo*. She facilitates creative writing workshops for Write Around Portland and coaches young writers for Playwrite, Inc.

Even before she knew how to form the letters of the alphabet, **Kristin Thiel** was "writing," dictating stories to her mom to put on paper. In 2006 she won the Elisabeth A. McPherson Award for Women Writers and earlier this year, the Ooligan Editors' Choice short story contest. When not writing fiction, Kristin works as an editor for Indigo Editing and serves as Community Outreach Director for Women in Portland Publishing. She's online at www.kristinthiel.com.

Hannah Thomassen finds inspiration as a poet and creative non-fiction writer in the Pacific Northwest landscape, where she lives a good life in the foothills of the Cascade Mountains with a husband, three sheep, three donkeys, a dozen chickens and a dog. Her poems have appeared or are forthcoming in *Verse-weavers*, *Big Bridge*, *Presence*, and in an anthology from Wising Up Press to be released Fall, 2007.

Wendy Thompson teaches writing through Saturday Academy and Portland Community College. She also taught literary arts for six years at the Vancouver School of Arts and Academics. Published in a variety of regional anthologies, Wendy has also won several poetry contests including a poetry slam at Portland State. With an MFA in dance, Ms. Thompson published professional articles in *Teaching Tolerance, Science & Children*, and *Impulse Journal*. She is currently pursuing certification in poetry/journal therapy.

l. franciszka voeltz is another way of saying 'fierce'. ms. fierce is a tangle of antique thread, a parchment paper moon rising over the city, a tarnished brass band marching down your street. she is a streak of hot pink heat, a holographic spill of glitter. her laugh lines are treasure maps in disguise. franciszka uses words to push back against the white supremacist capitalist patriarchy we live under. commiserate, communicate, collaborate: francesca_fire@riseup.net.

Victoria Wheeler continues to work part-time in education after retiring from Milwaukie High School. A writer of fiction, non-fiction, and poetry, she sometimes mines her journals, which she began in 1962, for material. Wife of Kevin and mother of Laura, a science teacher, she loves golfing, travel, and Portland's finest coffee shops. Victoria is the author of two books: *The Positive Teacher*, and *Daily Writing Topics Grades 7-12*, published by the Center for Learning.

Rhea Wolf writes a monthly astrology column (goddesstribe.com) as well as other dreamy, opinionated pieces of literature. She is the author of *Persephone Rising*, a self-published chapbook of poems and stories. She adores the rain, watching her daughter feed the chickens, hiking with her husband, talking about astrology and casting spells of fierce beauty.

Mary Zelinka lives in Albany, Oregon, and is the Assistant Executive Director at the Center Against Rape and Domestic Violence. Her writing is published in *Calyx, Crazy Woman Creek, The Sun,* and *Open Spaces*.

Ready to release your work into the VoiceCatcher pond?
Our nets will soon be out! Our 2008 submission window opens
February 1st—visit **www.pdxwomenwriters.com** in January
for more details. We look forward to hearing from you!